DREAM JUMPERS
THE INHERITANCE

First Printing, 2022

DREAM JUMPERS
the
INHERITANCE

WRITTEN AND
ILLUSTRATED
BY

Adrienne La Faye

TWELVE PUBLISHING LLC © 2022

DEDICATION

"I'm dedicating Dream Jumpers the Inheritance to every Child whose dreams haven't come to fruition, (yet). DREAM JUMPERS, the INHERITANCE, was created for kids just like you, to ignite your imaginations, to build better worlds, spaces where your best selves can exist."

"I can't forget the Adults who believe that the manifestations of their most brilliant selves have evaporated. Simply put, their time has passed. I protest because I believe it's never too late. My dreams guide me more today than they did when I was young. With age comes Wisdom."

"All People are born into the world with their life's purpose. However, family, society, gender bias, socioeconomics, etc., have dissuaded us from utilizing our passions. Daily Persevere to Reclaim Your True-Selves."

~Adrienne La Faye~

Contents

Dedication   iv

CHAPTER ONE
BEYOND HER COMPREHENSION   1

CHAPTER TWO
STUCK IN THE MIDDLE   9

CHAPTER THREE
SIGHTS UNSEEN   17

CHAPTER FOUR
THE PERVIOUS VAULT   25

CHAPTER FIVE
REAL-LIFE OR NIGHTMARES?   39

CHAPTER SIX
WAITING FOR PAPA'S RETURN   47

CHAPTER SEVEN
CUBE ASSIGNMENT   57

CHAPTER EIGHT
FALLING FROM GRACE   63

CHAPTER NINE
NO REDEMPTION FRIENDS   73

CHAPTER TEN
CAFETERIA FIGHTING CHALLENGE 77

CHAPTER ELEVEN
FIRST DAY AT THE ACADEMY 89

CHAPTER TWELVE
MR. POINSETTER'S CLASS 101

CHAPTER THIRTEEN
TEAM JUMPING 107

CHAPTER FOURTEEN
WRATHTORS: DEFENSE AND SPACE PODS 117

CHAPTER FIFTEEN
THEY'RE HERE! 127

CHAPTER SIXTEEN
ACTRESS NATALIE 133

CHAPTER SEVENTEEN
"TMI" (Too Much Information) 139

CHAPTER EIGHTEEN
UGH, THIS LITTLE GIRL 143

CHAPTER NINETEEN
BEING UNSURE 153

CHAPTER TWENTY
DOUBLE DODGE BALL 157

CHAPTER TWENTY-ONE
WE'RE IN BIG TROUBLE 165

CHAPTER TWENTY-TWO
PAPA'S LETTER AND HUMILIATION 171

CHAPTER TWENTY-THREE
SUNDAY SCHOOL   175

CHAPTER TWENTY-FOUR
YOU MUST GO BACK   183

CHAPTER TWENTY-FIVE
THE LIBRARY AND THE MANTRA   191

CHAPTER TWENTY-SIX
THE LAST ACT   195

CHAPTER TWENTY-SEVEN
THE FINAL TEST   199

CHAPTER TWENTY-EIGHT
NO WAY OUT   207

About The Author   222

CHAPTER
ONE

BEYOND HER
COMPREHENSION

"Malia, I need to talk to you," the voice echoed through her room.

"Why do you keep calling me?" She wondered.

"What do you want? Why won't you answer me?"

She tried to have a conversation with the Papa-like voice, but it only kept calling her name. This voice terrified her. It had haunted her for months. Or had it just been a few weeks? Malia shook her head. She was becoming more confused about what was real and what was not since Papa's passing.

"Malia, listen up, child. It is me, Papa. I need to talk to you now."

She said in a barely audible voice. "If you are my Papa, tell me where you are."

The teenager was in her room, staring out of the attic window; Malia watched a tornado-like formation of leaves on the roof fly up and scatter. The sun winked behind the midafternoon's spectacularly lit orange and yellow sky. However, the sun had disappeared in a moment, and the sky turned to a dark charcoal color with a lightning streak streaming downward as if someone had turned off a light switch.

Typically, Malia was a fierce child, but not when it came to hearing a voice she could not find. She gasped when she saw the sky change and forgot to exhale, and her heart stopped. The girl realized she had to breathe out so she wouldn't pass out. Malia has gone through a lot, it was not her first time watching the day turn to night in a matter of seconds, and she did not know why. She'd realized a while ago that the weather turned its worst every time her grandfather called to her. She was not sure it was his voice because he was dead. Right? But something or someone was calling her.

The voices had stopped.

That's it, Malia thought; she'd decided to find Papa, wherever he was hiding. The next time she heard his voice, she would hunt him down. And tonight was the night she'd wait for him. There was a bonus, her father was working late at the office tonight, and her brother Micah would be at Grand One's (their maternal grandmother) house. So, she'd wait for the voice and be ready to capture him.

Yes, tonight was the night; Malia crouched down on her knees, hidden behind the living room sofa. She waited as she restlessly anticipated the voice.

Suddenly, she heard the voice calling and sprang to her feet. "Malia, stop. Please, listen to me. Maliaaaa."

She ran toward the voice and jumped over the coffee table, both feet clearing it easily. She sidestepped a floor-to-ceiling lamp, her socks skidding on the wooden floor as she passed the dining room entrance. She grabbed the doorknob to stop it from sliding further.

"Where are you?" she screamed, "especially since you won't tell me who you are," she begged.

She heard the voice calling from upstairs. She headed towards the third-floor stairs, taking two stairs at a time, and abruptly stopped. She stood precisely in front of the closet door in the hallway. Her right hand quickly jerked the door open, and the left hand grasped as her body braced against the doorframe.

The tiny closet was empty. Malia could have sworn the voice was coming from inside the room. Silently Malia waited for the voice. As an athlete, she knew how to breathe quietly—breathing in and out, swallowing slowly not to make a sound so that the teenager could hear every creak in the house.

"Malia, I'm in here. Come through the door. Hurry up. You don't have much time."

The voice grew louder and reverberated off the ceiling. The girl could not pinpoint its direction. She was determined to find the sound, so she jumped on the stairs handrail and slid down like a fireman sliding down a fire pole.

She tiptoed through the house to the back porch and spied around. Malia tiptoed down to the basement and peered into the darkness. She thought IT was upstairs, so she quietly ran up the stairs back to the third floor. She heard nothing and checked the empty closet she'd jerked open minutes ago.

Malia waited as she stood on her tippy toes. Finally, her feet began to shake out of pure exhaustion. Her body slid down the wall to the floor, stopping as her back braced the staircase railing. The only sound she heard in the dead silence was swishing her blouse against the wall. The coolness of the wooden floor rose to reach her slumping body.

She used her hands to drag each leg as her house slippers scattered off her feet. She buried her head between her knees and rocked back and forth.

Her heart burst with pain from grief and loss, and she wept. Her tears splattered downward until the wetness clung to her clothes. Her grandfather had taught them everything they knew.

Like how to prepare for life if they'd find themselves alone. Malia wrestled. Maybe, Papa was torturing her because she had somehow let him down.

She knew Papa was dead, but her heart started to reason. What if He Is Alive? Yes, that's it; he was playing a joke, but that would be a cruel joke to play, and she shuddered from the thought.

Malia's sad and can't understand why she hears voices.
Illustration and Photography by Adrienne La Faye © 2022

Even though she was afraid, she kept asking the voice what it wanted, but it never responded. Slowly she stood, dragging her feet to her bedroom, and was relieved the room was across the hallway. Her naturally braided longer than shoulder-length hair swung, creating new hairstyles. She had mesmerizing eyes that would suck people in, wondering, who is this kid? Finally, she laid down on her bed.

Illustration and Photography by Adrienne La Faye

Underneath her breath, she whispered, "Help me to help you. Tell me how to find you." while she thought about her looks and how she compared to other girls her age. Since the twins were homeschooled, they did not have friends, and no other kids lived on their block or in their cul-de-sac. So, she'd searched online and stared into the permanent smiling faces of pretty girls on her laptop.

Malia saw herself as an average looking girl, maybe more than average; it was necessary that she not be too ugly, so she checked the mirror often. She was of average height, slender, and covered in perfect caramel brown skin. Malia clears her head by shaking it, and she says out loud, "focus."

Her twin Micah had to have heard the voice, too, she thought. She would ask him. Too tired, too scared to search anymore, Malia resigned herself to remembering the question her grandfather asked her entire life: Do you remember your gift?

CHAPTER
TWO

STUCK IN THE
MIDDLE

When Micah started hearing the voice, he innately thought his father was calling him, not his grandfather, Papa. He concluded that since it was a male voice, it had to be the man he refers to as the Father Figure. Micah believed the man wasn't good enough to be called Dad, and FF was more than the man deserved. Micah's search for the voice began last week when he entered his father's office. He crept slyly into the smoky room, leaned on the maroon overstuffed leather recliner, and tried to think of an excellent fake question to ask the father figure, but nothing came to mind. He knew if he asked the wrong question, his father would reprimand him.

There was that voice again. "Micah, it is me, Papa. I must talk to you." It would not go away. How could his grandfather call him when he was dead?

9

He fixed his eyes on his father's face behind the mahogany desk. His father was a stern, mean-looking man, tall and thin, whose work clothes were always crisp and clean, even at home.

Micah would tuck his head into his shoulders to block the volume of the father's voice. Now he nervously tapped his foot against the bottom of the chair. Nothing. Not even a twitch from the man.

"Micah, son, I have to talk to talk to you." It wasn't his father speaking. Micah spun around. Who was calling his name? He grabbed his stomach with both hands as it made gurgling noises.

His eyes rolled up into his head. He was always hungry, but not this time. No, it was not hunger. It was raw fear that filled his abdomen. He refused to show his emotions.

There must be a scientific reason for these voices, Micah thought. His fingers dug for his notepad in the side pocket of his cargo shorts, and he wrote:

1. **Not Father's voice.**
2. **It's probably Papa's voice, but how?**
3. **Research ghosts and beyond the dead.**

He wiped the beads of sweat from his brow and rubbed the wetness on his shorts. No matter how bad it got, he would not ask his father for guidance. Instead, his father would say, "Boy, face your fears and be a man." His father never helped him with anything unless it was by accident.

Micah sat in the recliner and whispered, "ouch" when the chair's leather pinched the skin on his back thighs. He grasped the armrests with both hands to position his legs, so the bottom of his shorts would be on the seat rather than on his skin. Losing his balance, his right hand slipped off the armrest, and the boy's gigantic sixteen-size shoes smacked hard against the wooden floor. He froze, waiting for his father to react to his presence. He glanced at his father. Was he going to yell at him?

So cool. It was going to be one of those days when the man would ignore him. Micah sat and waited as he looked outside the window close to the chair.

Often daydreamed of the possibility that his father wasn't his father, and somehow the twins had been secretly stolen at birth. How else could he sanely deal with his father's hatred for him?

Micah had the same skin color and height as his sister, and he was a boy version of her. However, he walked with his upper body tilted backward to keep balanced because his feet were too big for him. His hair had these incredible dark browns, blondes, and reds, all mixed in a short Afro. He had the same eyes, but they did not have the same effect on people. He had anxiously waited for the chance to stand up to their parent but also knew why he didn't. The man would pin him down to the floor and make him beg to be released. He disliked him more daily.

He flinched, moved closer to the windows, and was surprised by what he had just seen. The evening's sun crept through the Venetian blinds. Hues of orange, yellow, pink, and red across the skyline reflected off the white slats and warmed the room's atmosphere. Micah knew earlier in the day that something was wrong because he'd watched lightning crackle across the dark gray sky, like in horror movies. He wiped his sweaty palm on the sleeve of his shirt and jotted down:

4. Why is the weather affected too?

He let out a sigh of relief as he sunk further into the recliner.

Micah's worried about how the house feels and sounds.
Illustration and Photography by Adrienne La Faye © 2022

The smell of burnt tobacco from his father's pipe swirled up close to Micah's nose and snapped the boy back from his thoughts. A picture of President Barack Obama hung directly behind the desk. His father's inspiration was to become the first black man to accomplish something big at his firm. Micah refused to be like his father. The man never won a trial. He did not have the guts to face a jury because he would freeze every time.

Father had steadily groomed Micah from an early age to choose a career. This summer, he and Malia are turning thirteen, and the adult clock is ticking louder. They are both expected to get jobs in high school and leave home after graduation. Their father blamed them for their mother's death, and Micah has always planned to get away ASAP. He knew they weren't ready.

As Micah thought about leaving home, the anger grew inside him. He expanded his chest with air and gripped the arms of the chair. Its legs wobbled against the wooden floor. He sneered at his father, who never once looked up from his paperwork. Micah's tongue was so dry he could barely swallow his spit. He didn't know how he would leave, but he would figure it out.

His nose flared in and out. That's it, he thought. I'm done with this man. His long, gangly feet banged on the floor as he vaulted from the chair to leave. His hand grasped the doorknob, the door flew open, and he collided with his twin.

"Hi, Daddy." His sister's eyes were bulging, and she was breathing rapidly. "Hey, Micah, whatcha y'all doing?"

Micah staggered from the sudden collision, and he saw fear in her eyes.

Father looked at his watch, ignoring their strange behavior. "It's dinner time. Go wash your hands and stop being so loud."

Micah watched Malia spin, rotating on the tips of her house slippers. Her hair slapped in her mouth and stuck to her lips. She paused, instinctively spat it out, and swept it off her face. Micah could see she was worried about the breathtaking sunset that had returned, flooding the room through the blinds.

"What's going on? Why did you bust into Father's office?" Micah asked, even though he didn't want to talk about it.

Malia pulled her brother close to her. "Micah, we must talk. There are some crazy, weird things happening," she whispered. "Are you blind? Haven't you noticed the weather?"

They walked down the dark hallway toward the kitchen. Micah stumbled over their dog, TJ's plastic toy, and fell against the wall. His toys were scattered around the house.

Malia continued, "The sky goes from sunny to dark in nanoseconds."

"Why are you whispering?" Micah pretended not to have a clue about what had just happened outside.

She dropped her voice even lower and moved closer to Micah. "Brother, things are happening that I can't explain. Don't tell me you haven't heard anything strange."

Their father called out to them before Micah had a chance to respond. "Hey, Malia! Where is the food that Grand One sent over last night?" He shouted out loud because FF's head was buried in the fridge. He was always so demanding when he spoke to them. He pulled out the collard greens and ribs and set the cold containers on the kitchen counter for Malia to warm up. She had to prepare dinner every night.

The bones went in the microwave first. Father always expected her to fix his plate, too.

"Set the table, now," he snapped. "Micah, get the plates!"

Micah said, calmly enunciating each word through clenched teeth, "I already got them. I live here, too, you know. So, stop telling me what to do." Micah placed each plate on the kitchen table in their assigned places, including utensils and napkins.

Micah told himself not to lose his temper. He watched as Malia pressed the microwave buttons to warm the ribs and waited for the collard greens to heat to a low bubble.

The microwave beeped off, and she cooked the potato salad only to take off the chill. The twins spied their father in the microwave reflection as he left the kitchen. Malia quickly turned to Micah.

"Haven't you heard any weird things lately?"

Micah placed a single finger against his lips, signaling silence.

Father returned with his laptop and sat at the head of the table. The microwave beeped, and Malia pulled out the potato salad. The family moved like a well-oiled machine with barely a sound.

The sweet aroma of soul food filled the small yellow kitchen from the ceiling to the shiny yellow-blue checkered floor.

Micah sat down and welcomed the silence as he dug into his meal. He was still upset by the voice, and his mind wrestled with the silent treatment from his father with his domineering mood.

Micah caught sight of his twin out of his peripheral vision. Malia was twirling her collards with her fork; her eyes were thoughtlessly watching Father read something on his computer while eating dinner.

The girl turned her attention back to her food, repeatedly picking at the greens on her plate. Micah could sense that her nerves were acting up because she wasn't eating anything.

She fixed her stare on Micah and made grunting noises. His eyes quickly darted back to his plate, looking innocent and unaware.

"Humph, humph, humph," she spewed out with disgust. Micah knew what his sister was doing, but he ignored her. Her grunt is a learned sound from their grandparents. It was commonly used when one was not pleased.

Most Black folks use this sound when upset about something or something that seems incredible. Grand One told the twins that during the days of slavery, the slaves were not allowed to express their true feelings to their masters, so they would hum in low voices, humph, humph, and humph. The phrase has three succinct humphs to signal displeasure.

Micah could feel his sister's scorching stare on him now. He figured she wondered how he could eat at a time like this. She always said he ate as though he had existed on Vietnam War rations for years and never had enough to eat. She had read about the war in U.S. history class.

"Obotauk!" was Malia's signal to Micah that they needed to talk. They'd had a secret language since birth but hardly used it now. Instead, she pulled out all kinds of tricks from her arsenal to get his attention.

Micah looked past her and dug his fork into a mound of potato salad, which fell onto his shirt. He licked it off. He was defiantly making her wait until after dinner to talk to him.

"Micah, wash the dishes," Father mumbled and left the room. "Brother, in my room when you finish," Malia ordered as she pointed her index finger upward. Micah nodded and shoveled another forkful of collards into his mouth.

CHAPTER
THREE

SIGHTS UNSEEN

Micah tapped once on his sister's bedroom door. She opened it just enough to allow him to squeeze through before shutting it quickly behind him. The room's windows gave her a complete view from the front of the house to the back. Beneath each of the windowsills were built-in bookcases that nestled the length of the oblong room.

Micah's room was just like her room but in reverse. Malia's office was on the right side of the grand house, and Micah's room was on the left.

His eyes scanned the wall of Malia's collection of Serena Williams' posters, the famous G.O.A.T. tennis player. Serena was her idol. Malia's goal was to be the best athlete, too.

On her dresser sat a picture of their mother. Micah had seen Malia routinely embrace the old photo, kiss her mother's mouth, and finger trace her face and hair. She did this every time she entered her room. Yet, Malia refused to forget mama.

Grand One always said that Malia was the perfect likeness of her mom. So convinced she would meet their mother again one day.

"Let's go outside to the garage," Micah said. "We don't want him to hear any of this." Malia agreed.

They silently tiptoed down the barely lit stairs, side by side, trying their best not to let their father hear them. Their little dog, T.J., followed behind. Of course, Micah's big feet in his shoes just had to thud against the wall along the staircase.

They froze in place and waited and listened. The twins did not hear a thing, so they kept moving. Finally, they snuck quietly out to not provoke an interrogation by their father.

The old house seemed to creak louder than ever as they crept into the living room. Family photos in frames of varying shapes and sizes lined the walls and fireplace mantel of the old house.

They edged through the foyer, the formal dining room, and the kitchen. T.J. He barked as soon as they made it to the back porch. Micah scooped up the dog and grabbed his muzzle to keep him quiet. It worked.

The twins quietly closed the screen door and darted from the back porch as though their lives depended on it, escaping unseen by their father. Micah held T.J. tightly to his chest. They stopped at the old, ragged garage burrowed behind the newer, bigger one from the big house.

Micah noticed how the full moon lit up the dark sky and how the aroma of freshly cut grass permeated the evening air. A few droplets of rain fell onto their noses and cheeks.

T.J. growled and squirmed against Micah's tight hold on him. "Shush," he whispered into the dog's ear. Malia gently pulled open the door of the old forgotten garage to prevent its hinges from squeaking too loudly in the silent night.

They entered the dark garage. Malia turned around and slowly closed the door. She turned on the lights, but Micah instantly slammed them off. In his left side pocket was a flashlight so the Father Figure wouldn't see them (F.F.), in case light might illuminate more brightly than most nights.

They maneuvered through old junk to the back wall and huddled closely together. The garage smelled old and dusty. Micah turned on the flashlight he'd hidden in his pocket and held T.J. with the other with one hand.

"Sis, I'm not sure this is the best place for us to be after all." Micah peered around the dimly lit garage, sniffing the fumes from the lawn mower gas can and watching suspicious shadows moving across the walls of the small structure. "It's a horrible idea to be out here. You know anything could get us."

"Don't trip. It's all good," Malia said. "No more dodging and fooling around, now. Answer me honestly." She stared straight into his eyes, "Micah, are you hearing voices that sound like Papa?"

"Yasss, are you too?" He was so shocked a hand flew up to his mouth, stopping a shout from escaping while nodding in disbelief.

"Why didn't you say something? You must be kidding me! Did you hear the voices too? You saw me trying to get your attention at dinner.

"What is wrong with you, dude?" Malia rambled in exasperation. "Why were you avoiding my question?"

Micah gently cowered T.J. onto the floor. The dog growled. The garage door was now closed, and they were far enough from the house so no one could hear the dog.

"I didn't mention anything because I thought I was going crazy. I didn't want to scare you. But honestly, tonight was the first time I knew I wasn't tripping, and the voice was real."

"Whew, okay, okay. That makes sense." She instantly forgave him.

Micah exhaled to calm down. "I tried to figure out what was going on."

"Micah," Malia's voice quivered. "I'm scared. Why are we hearing him? Moreover, what does he want? Maybe we are both going crazy." Malia pouted her lips; tears puddled in her eyes. "I can't believe you didn't say something, and you still wouldn't have if I didn't insist that we talk. We used to talk about everything. So, what's going with us?"

"Malia, you need to stop looking like that," Micah tried to calm her down.

"Like what?"

"Like you are scared out of your mind."

She propped her head in her hand, resting on her knee, and stared at him.

Micah changed his approach. He tried to be more reassuring. "I mean, try not to be too scared. We will figure this out together, okay?"

"Boy, please, you're scared more than me." She refused to dwell on uncertainties, so she returned to the point.

Micah did not like arguing with her, and to tell the truth, he had doubts.

"I'm not afraid," he snapped. "I think showing anger and fighting is stupid and juvenile. However, don't get it twisted. I'm nobody's punk."

"I don't know how much more I can take hearing that creepy voice. Maybe we should find someone who can help us." Malia, in full throttle, rambled on.

Suddenly the twins noticed how strangely T.J. was acting. First, he started barking and fixed his gaze on the wall. Finally, his ears stood straight up, and he let out a long, slow growl. His teeth gnarled in anger or fright. It was hard for them to tell.

Then he paced in circles until he turned himself directly into the wall. He sniffed at the floor and then stood on the door on his front legs. Incessantly, he kept barking at the back wall. He looked as though he was trying to dig something out.

Micah watched T.J.'s strange behavior. His eyes became cold and fixated on the wall where T.J. was scratching. He was in a trance. He could see through the wall beyond the garage like an open window. Then he stopped. He stood in a fight mode, and now T.J. began barking frantically, turning in panicked circles. Micah questioned what he was seeing. Then, it started to take shape. It was an image. He could hear Malia talking and T.J. barking. As the vision became clear, they were drowned out and back into distant sounds.

Micah spiraled into the middle of a dream where he could see things happening. He sensed everything was off, as though he were watching a movie. He saw Papa but could not hear what he was saying. Papa was talking and laughing with Auntie Thelma. He and Malia were there, too.

They were all sitting around a table, cheerfully eating a delicious dinner. Micah could smell the aromas, and his mouth began to water for a bit of whatever they were eating. But, as always, he was hungry.

Suddenly, a trumpet loudly blew out a "Da da, da da."

The ground beneath them started to rumble. It was an earthquake! It shook the table where they were eating dinner. Papa, Auntie Thelma, and he and Malia were all catapulted in the same direction and started flying around.

Then, another trumpet bellowed. Papa, Auntie Thelma, and the table with all its delightful food instantly vanished! It was just him and his sister, alone, flying around in the air. Then darkness took over this dream.

Micah could see that he was hollering at his sister. "They're going to kill us! We've gotta get out of here, now!"

However, it was too late. Something had captured Malia. Micah could do nothing but watch them drag her along a green road and down into a dark gray sky.

Micah was startled from this dream or vision he was experiencing and jumped to his feet. He began to shout, "Sis, use your super strength! Break free, and fly!"

T.J. lay down on the dirty floor of the old garage, but he continued to stare at the wall.

"Whoa, you need to sit down," said Malia. "Are you okay? Are you sick or something? Why were you looking so weird, and what's with T.J.?"

Micah hugged himself as tightly as he could. Malia scooped up T.J. His growls turned to pants as her hold comforts him. She could feel T.J.'s heart beating rapidly. "Micah, tell me what just happened to you."

Micah's legs shook. They felt like rubber bands. Malia led him back to the rusty metal stool to catch his breath. The vision emotionally drained Micah.

He was now fully aware of his surroundings. He could distinctly hear the rain beating on the garage windows as T.J. panted and his sister spoke.

"Sis, you know I have always had crazy dreams, right?" He stared into space, although out of his trance, trying to explain what he had just seen.

She nodded. "Yea, yea, but—this—one—was—different."

"Yes, it was different. I know I should've told you sooner. I was going to tell you, but I had to do my research first."

Micah was settling down. His breathing returned to normal, and he could now speak and tell his sister everything he saw.

"This time, I could hear you talking to me, but I couldn't move. Then your voice and T.J.'s growling faded into a distant noise.

This vision was way more intense than the others." He explained his dream to his wide-eyed sister.

"Flying?" Malia asked cautiously. "Do you mean like birds or like angels?"

"Not like either," he said, "Something was holding us up." "What does that mean?" she grilled him.

"I swear! I don't know what it means," he said, his hands waving defensively. "I can't explain it, but it's happening for a reason."

"Micah, are you okay? You scared me. I didn't know what to do. Promise me from now on you'll tell me when you had or are having one," she demanded. "Promise now me, Micah."

"I promise to tell you about the visions," he said with sincerity, adding, "You need to chill."

"Boy, I don't know what I would have done if you hadn't come out of it!" she exclaimed. "What would I tell Grand One or Dad? I didn't know what was happening. You were acting all weird, and T.J. was going nuts. So, of course, I'm upset!"

"Now it's your turn to promise me that you won't tell a single soul about any of this."

She swore to secrecy.

"You know everybody will think we're crazy, so tell no one," He urged. "I mean NO ONE. I'm going to investigate as much as possible, okay?"

Malia nodded rapidly.

"I agree, brother. I'm wit' choo."

"Let's get back inside before he misses us." That was all he needed to know. They were working together, and they were not crazy.

Well, that was what he hoped.

Micah locked one arm through his sister's, still feeling out of sorts, while she held T.J. with the other. She expertly guided them back through the creaking maze of the house without a peep said between them. T.J.'s head rested on Malia's shoulder.

Malia softly closed her door just in the nick of time. Their father hollered at the top of his lungs. "Micah, clean your room now and finish picking up your mess! Also, Malia! You are not getting out of this either! So, this time clean your room well, or you will be punished. That means no running on that track, no internet, and no books!"

They paused and asked if he said anything about them sneaking inside from the garage. Because this was not their usual behavior, he would suspect they were doing something wrong.

Micah whispered, "Act right so he won't be suspicious."

"Don't worry, I got this," She smiled big. "But, Dad, my room isn't that dirty." All the while, she was secretly laughing at his usual reaction. "Besides, we have too much stuff to do. Can't we do it tomorrow?" Malia pretended to plead.

She smirked as she watched her brother robotically leave her room and walk across the hallway to his room. He held T.J. and placed him on his bed, then began to put his things in order.

Their father rarely talked to Micah unless it was to order him around. Now that she thought about it, he didn't speak to her that much either.

"No, I do not want any arguments from you, girl," yelled their father. "Your room is the worst. Just clean up your mess NOW." Under her breath, Malia said, "Shoot, that was way too close.

CHAPTER
FOUR

THE PERVIOUS
VAULT

Malia sat upstairs in the darkness of her closet, poking her hand around the floor. TJ panted from the heat of the small, enclosed space. She moved a tennis shoe from under her hand and nudged closer to her dog. At last, she could feel his paw and yanked his collar to pull him closer, but she had to scoot in to get closer to him.

He shook his leg loose from her grasp and squirmed further away from her. TJ was again on the loose, trying to avoid another bath. She thought if TJ hated a bath so much, she would let it slide for now and be his comrade. She scooted in even closer, but her body lunged forward with brute force hitting her head against the back wall. She straightened and repositioned her body, lifting a hand to rub the sore spot. Her hands found TJ. She picked him up and sat him on her lap.

She sat in the closet with TJ, trying to forget about the previous day in the garage, when she noticed a feel cool air lightly blowing against the side of her face. It was coming from somewhere in the closet. It was hot in there, so the cool breeze felt nice.

"Look, TJ, you're off the hook for tonight. Let us make a truce." Malia put out her hand palm up, and he laid his paw in her hand. She hugged him and nuzzled him on his neck and behind his ears. It was then Malia saw a sliver of a hole. She had never noticed it, considering the countless times she had been in that closet.

Wait, is this a door? She thinks.

It was sealed tight with paint and nails, but she could still move it smoothly. She had always been super strong her entire life. It was one of her best gifts.

Their father refused to talk to the twins about their unique abilities, but that was how he handled most things. He knew they weren't like other children. She believed, secretly, that he was ashamed of them. The twins didn't talk about it with each other, either. They accepted who they were.

Malia pushed lightly against the wall, and it opened before her. It was a door to a never-before-seen hidden room. She felt guilty for a second, using her ability of strength, but no one was around, so she dismissed the feeling.

Malia crawled through the kid-sized opening. TJ cautiously sniffed around the door's opening, and then he did a low crawl into the room. He was an American Eskimo, and his white coat glowed in the dark room.

THE CLEARING: Papa explains everything, well, almost everything.

Illustration and Photography by Adrienne La Faye © 2022

TJ stopped sniffing. He lay down contently. Man, this is the spot. At least that is what Malia imagined, he thought, patting his back. The twins believed they knew what TJ was thinking, and they would interpret for him as if he were a human. But, of course, in their hearts, he was human.

Malia blinked her eyes rapidly to adjust to the smidgeon of light that barely lit the closet. She picked up a dusty old fashion toy truck that was kicked onto its side when she entered the secret room. She loved the scaled-down table and its four matching chairs. There was a little girl's tea set in the middle of the tiny table.

Malia turned around in slow circles, looking from one side of the room to the other. Across from her, in the corner, was a model train set. It was on top of another table with one chair pushed beneath it.

It reminded her of the toys in Grand One's childhood pictures. The room had an aura of a time that had long passed. She tried to imagine the kids who played in this room. What had happened to them? Malia had never seen anything like this in her life.

"Micah! Micah, come in here! Micaaah, get in here now!"

TJ let out a bark. He constantly barked when someone called a family member else because he was helping to alert the person, too.

"Malia, where are you?" "I'm in here!" she shouted.

"Where is here? I am in your room, and I hear you, but I can't see you. Keep talking."

"Come into my closet and get down on your hands and knees, and then you'll see me. Hurry, I just found the best surprise, everrrrrr in the world!"

She watched as he entered her closet. First, he hunched down and stepped clumsily on her dress shoe with his right foot, lost his balance on his left foot, and both of his big feet slid out from under him. Then, out of sheer preservation, his skinny arms thrashed around to grasp a handful of clothes hanging from the clothing rod.

It all seemed to be happening in slow motion as he tried to stabilize himself, but his body wavered until he sprawled out on a bumpy row of shoes. He lay there to catch his breath, pushing off a blouse that landed on his head. Malia laughed at him, and he smiled, too.

Now that he was on the floor, he could see through the small door. Malia sat on the little kid's chair. He crawled on his hands and knees into the tiny room. "What in the world . . . What is? How did you find it?" Micah was speechless

Malia saw the amazement in his eyes. Micah turned his head, and his eyes roamed the room. Malia noticed another door within this secret room as she watched her brother's bewildered face.

"Look, there's another door!" Malia pointed towards the opposite wall. "It's gotta go somewhere else!" TJ began to scratch the wall with his paw as though something lay beyond it.

"Maybe it goes into my room?" Micah repositioned himself, sitting on his legs and feet, and pushed hard on the door.

"Malia, you push the door."

Malia crawled over and easily pushed open the door. There was a stairwell with five steps up, then led five stairs down into the closet in his bedroom.

Micah said, "I think this stairwell was built over the hallway so it could go into my room."

"Da, you think?"

"Well, I think so. This room is the coolest place in the world. Let's not tell anybody about this," Micah said. "It is our secret place." "We can hide here, and no one can find us or hear us. SCORE."

They high-five.

Malia found an old, yellowed picture on the floor. "Micah, who are these people?"

There were about forty-five or fifty children of various ages sitting on a dirt lawn. They looked like they may have been slaves. They stared at the photo. "Our family," they said in unison.

"What should we name the room?" Malia wondered aloud.

"It has to be THE VAULT because it was closed up like at the bank," Micah answered. "There must be something precious in "Some of those folks are our family, and some are friends." Again, it was the voice, and this time both twins heard it and were paralyzed with fear.

TJ heard the voice. He sat straight with ears pointed forward. His eyes glared straight ahead at the wall, and his tail slowly began to wag.

"Finally, you found the vault. It---is---about---time!"

Malia was about to bolt up and out of the vault when suddenly the voice spoke again.

"Malia, Micah, don't Y'all remember my voice? It's Papa."

A faint figure slowly appeared across the tiny table, but the vision was tuning in and tuning out with horizontal lines flickering up and down, just like an old TV screen.

Micah whispered to Malia, "Do you see what I see?" "Yeah, I think . . . it kind of looks like a man, doesn't it?"

Malia stood frozen in her spot as she beheld a sight she had never seen. She gathered the courage to stay in the room as she saw Micah's body rise from the floor and was gently placed down onto his feet. He twisted and turned frantically to scramble out of there. Then, snap! His legs swung up into the air, his torso hit the floor like a bag of potatoes, and his head hit hard against the wall behind him.

Without hesitation, he hollered, "I'm out of this ghost trap. Let's get out of here!" He motioned for her to come.

He turned and scurried out on his hands and knees at a rabbit's pace, making a rhythmic thumping noise to exit the room. Thump, thump, thump. Thump, thump, thump.

After clambering for about twenty feet, Micah stopped to look back towards the door, expecting his sister to be right behind him, but instead, he saw the man. His image was brighter than it was a few seconds ago. Micah's eyes popped wide open.

Malia saw her grandfather, too. He had changed from when he was alive. He looked younger and slimmer.

"Malia! What are you doing?" Micah was insistent. "Let's get out of here! It's a trap!"

TJ barked excitedly, but the bark was not a warning bark like in the garage. No, it was more like an "I'm glad to see you" bark.

"Shush, it looks just like Papa. Will you wait a minute?" Malia snapped back at her brother. She slowly began to enunciate each of her words. "You—sound—like—Papa—but—how—do—we—know--you're—him-? Besides, our Papa is dead."

Malia looked back at her brother to get his approval. She then gave him a wink to let him know she had this, and she was not afraid.

"I have to find out what's going on." Her neck cracked as she turned back to face the wall and shouted, "Okay, okay, we get that you're a ghost, but I'm tired of this crap, show yourself!"

Malia kept a watch on her brother. She would follow him if necessary, but she saw that Micah did not know what to do. He was stuck kneeling by the door. She looked toward TJ, who stayed with her, but he seemed happy.

Out of nowhere, a crisp ZAP ZUP ZIP sound reverberated off the walls and echoed inside the vault. Both twins involuntary screamed.

"Whaaat! Ooooh, no!" Their voices echoed inside the tiny room at the same time.

A dark-skinned man appeared across the tiny table from where the twins sat. It was Papa. An average weight, thick mustache, and a large bald graying strip of hair circled the back of his head from ear to ear.

Malia thought, he looks like Papa. However, then she smelled the familiar cologne he had always worn. That was all Malia needed she was convinced that he was her Papa. Malia jumped up and ran to Papa, giving him a giant hug, letting Papa's arms engulf her.

"Papa, I've missed you so much." She loved Papa more than anyone and would do anything to make him happy. When he was alive, she used to spend most of her time with him. "So, it was you calling me all this time! Why didn't you? Oh, right, you did keep saying you were

Papa. I couldn't find you. Where were you hiding?"

"Y'all had to find the room before I could show myself. I couldn't take the risk. I can only show myself to you and Micah."

"Okay, it's cool. I'm happy you are here."

Papa reached down to pet TJ, who was turning in circles with excitement, barking happily and jumping upon him. Papa picked him up and sat him on the table in front of him.

Malia wanted her brother to believe, too.

"Boy, get on over here and stop playing like you don't know me," Papa joked.

Micah was still on the floor, but at Papa's request, he inched toward him and stuck out his right arm to shake his hand. Papa grabbed Micah's hand and pulled him up into the tightest bear hug possible. Unfortunately, the boy did not return the hug.

Papa cleared his throat before he spoke. "Y'all sit down. Before we do anything else, I must tell you what's going on here and give you the rules. No. Before I tell y'all anything, I want to know about your Grand One. How is my sweet Annie doing?"

Malia's heart burst with sadness, and she began to weep. Micah answered the senior man.

"Grand One is great. Don't you worry about her, Papa"?

That must have been all that he needed. The old man paused for a few more seconds and pulled out a handkerchief to wipe his tears and brow. TJ jumped down on the floor and lay by his feet, and fell asleep.

Papa took a moment and then looked directly at Micah. The old man's expression said everything. Trust me. I'm here to help you.

Malia could not tell if her brother was convinced.

Papa started over, explaining his visit to the closet. "I was not allowed to reveal the truth until I transitioned to my new life, and you both had to be ready.

I know, Micah, you have dreams that you cannot decipher whether they are real or fake."

Micah nodded yes.

"What y'all are experiencing is a phenomenon. It is one of the greatest gifts in the world. I'm here to teach y'all exactly how to transition between two worlds, and I have a concise time to help y'all."

Micah mumbled, "How did you know I had dreams?"

Malia's mouth twisted into a frown, and she blurted out. "How can you exist in two worlds?"

Their grandfather said gently and deliberately, "It can be done, sweetie, it can be done."

She asked in a hushed tone, "Papa, why can't you stay with us? If you can move between two worlds, why aren't you with Grand One? But, Papa, is this a dream? Can you go from one world to another whenever you want? How long have you been doing this?"

"What is the number one question that I've always asked y'all?" Papa said.

"Do you remember your gift? We are all born into the world with a gift. You have everything you need to be who you are authentic." Papa answered his question before either one could.

"See, I knew you'd remember what I told you." Papa was proud. He continued to explain the other world. "I am a Dream Jumper, and I can jump into anyone's sleep to help guide them toward their finding their purpose in life."

Malia saw that Micah now believed. So, she asked, "Can we do this, too?"

Micah nodded. "Yes, we can." Micah didn't know how he knew it, but somehow, he just did...

"So, you do get it now, Micah?"

"Yes, it's making sense."

"So here are the rules of the law," Papa began to explain the fundamentals of Dream Jumping. "Yes, Malia, you both will be Dream Jumpers. Auntie Thelma and I were given the gift from our grandmamma at the same age you are now, and just like you all are receiving the gift from me.

It's a requirement to transfer the gift only to grandchildren." He paused. "The gift is passed down to every other generation and is only intended for fraternal boy and girl twins.

It must be a boy and girl set because the female and male viewpoints are essential to keep the balance and to help children who face challenges that may be common only to their gender. Your legacy is jumping children.

Many of our ancestors have been Jumpers. I thanked God when y'all were born. I've been waiting for the day that I could guide you to your dream journey.

Papa continued while the twins stayed silent and in awe of what they are hearing. "You cannot grasp everything in one night. It will take education, training, and a lifetime of trial and error to master your gifts."

Micah interjected. "I knew the visions were for a reason, and this confirms I'm not crazy." Then Micah prodded Papa with questions. "How can we help kids? How can we help when we don't know anything, and we're kids too?"

"Yes, yes, those are good questions."

Malia can tell her Papa was a little nervous. He slowly stood up from the tiny table and placed his hands in his pants pockets, and the ceiling automatically expanded to make room for his height. The children watched in amazement as the walls magically re-adjusted for his size, and for a fleeting moment, she saw Micah in their grandfather.

"That is right. There is a reason for all of this," Papa repeated. "How we help children is by jumping into their dreams."

Papa decided it would be best if he kept seated for the rest of his explanation. He had a lot to tell them. He slipped his hands out of his pockets, sat down, and rested his elbows on his knees. The ceiling morphed back to its original height. He paused in thought, looking at the twins and rubbing his hands together. He had to pace himself so he would not leave out any significant information.

All this felt weird and right to Malia at the same time.

Papa began to talk. "Most children don't follow their dreams. It is not because they don't want to, but it is because they are discouraged from acknowledging their true passions. Many parents don't agree with their child's career choice.

Some single parents work too much and would love to give them everything, but they can't because they're too poor. Also, some parents can completely ignore their children."

Their father did not spend time with them, either. That thought rang through both twins' minds. "A Dream Jumper's purpose is to help those kids find a way to fulfill their destiny, whatever the reason."

Malia looked at her twin and saw in his expression that he, too, realized that they were like the children they were going to help. Micah's head hung down, and he made angry fists with both hands. Malia wiped her nose with the back of her hand. That truth is all too real for them, and it hurt.

"Now, listen to me closely," Papa cautioned. "Be extremely careful. There is an entire evil species out there whose only mission is to kill all Dream Jumpers.

Their only job is to stop us from Dream Jumping." He hesitated. "They're called Wrathtors. They're our enemies, and you'll have to fight them one day. We all must fight them. So, do y'all understand? How do y'all feel about your gift?" Now it was Papa's turn to anticipate their answers.

"No," said Micah. "How do we jump into dreams?"

"Son, some things I must show you. It's better than telling y'all."

Both kids nodded their heads, and together they said, "Yes, we get it. We can't wait to become Dream Jumpers."

TJ raised his head and looked at Malia. He was her protector.

"There y'all go again, saying the same thing at the same time." Papa laughed and smiled. "I must go now. It is almost midnight and way past your bedtime." He stood up to leave and the ceiling again adjusted for his height.

Malia would have objected to him leaving, but tonight they were exhausted. She could see Micah's eyelids were half open. Their minds spun with the new information and with excitement for their new lives.

Malia yawned and asked, "When will we see you again?" TJ stretched his hind legs, kicking one leg out at a time.

"I'm still a Dream Jumper." Papa smiled. "I Jump adult dreamers who realize later in life they need to be happy and need guidance on how to make their passions real.

I have an assignment that calls for my immediate attention, so I will not be available until Thursday night. I will see you both here at the same time. Don't forget. I will be back. Be ready. Your training will not start until I return, so use this time to make sense of your gifts."

He walked over to them, kissed them both on their foreheads, and patted TJ's head. "Whoa, I almost forgot. Y'all can never tell anyone who or what you are." Then he vanished.

CHAPTER
FIVE

REAL-LIFE OR
NIGHTMARES?

The twins both had nightmares that night. They fell asleep and instantly entered the R.E.M. dream state. Micah walked by himself through a tunnel and saw his sister in the shaft, too. They were both frightened. He shoved his hands deep in his pockets, trying to keep them warm. In this dream, Micah was aware that he was dreaming.

Whoosh! An enormous being, a thing, flew out in front of him, about thirty feet away. It headed straight at him and then quickly whooshed past. He turned to run away, but as usual, his size-sixteen feet stuck to the ground. He tried moving his legs and feet by clutching his shorts with his hands while keeping his eyes pinned to where he had seen the thing.

He feverishly persisted and finally ripped his left foot off the wet pavement. He needed to run away but tripped over his right foot, stuck to the ground. He grabbed the ankle of his right foot and yanked it with all his might. Ugh! He fell slightly backward. He was free!

He ran faster than ever before in his life. Fear took over where his limited physical ability could not, and he ran in the opposite direction of the thing. It seemed he had been running forever but slowed his pace to use his jacket sleeve to wipe his sweaty face and runny nose. He heard the slow clamber of footsteps on the wet ground in the silence as they approached from behind.

He began to tremble and yelled, "DANG, whoever or whatever you are, you better leave me alone!" He continued running fast, away from the thing and footsteps. He could not seem to run fast enough. SLAP! SLAP! SLAP! SLAP! The sound banged inside his head. Just as the steps picked up their pace and moved closer to him, they suddenly stopped. The silence was deafening. His ears rang. So, he halted too.

Micah's breathing was labored, and his heart raced. He hunched over with his hands on his knees, barely able to catch his wind. He saw his breath in the cold, stagnant air. It looked like smoke blowing out of a chimney.

He was using his eyes to see visions in a new way. The images usually came to him, and he watched them like a movie. Instead, this vision came to him, and he was in it. He could not gather his thoughts to decipher what was happening because fear gripped him. He stayed hunched over in a resting position catching his breath. He looked down for just a moment, but as he looked up toward the tunnel, he saw a sliver of light. He blinked his eyes several times to adjust his sight. Finally, the boy looked behind, and the light glimmered brighter.

He saw his sister. His twin was running, too, but he could not pinpoint her location in the tunnel. It was dark and hard to adjust his eyesight, and Malia ran scared.

His breathing settled, so he began to run again to find Malia. He saw she held her arms close to stay warm. She walked quickly and then stopped. Micah watched her expression change. She was making a questioning face. Her eyes darted from left to right. Had she heard something behind her? She listened, tilting her head ever so slightly to pick up any sounds around her.

She then bolted with lightning speed. Malia was not only healthy, but she was a superfast runner. He watched her run incredibly fast and saw that she was aware of her surroundings inside the tunnel. Her hair was wet, and water from the tunnel ceiling showered down onto the top of her head. She kept running as the tunnel water trickled down her face and into her eyes. She repeatedly blinked to push the water from her eyelids and lashes.

Her vision was now in focus. She was frightened as she came face-to-face with a dark ghost-like figure. It sneered at her. In mid-stride, her feet slid out in front of her like a baseball player sliding past the first baseman. She stopped abruptly, making two long wet streaks on the tunnel floor with her feet. She righted herself, spun around, and ran in the opposite direction faster than before.

Micah still ran, too. He could even see his sister. Surely by now, he thought, she should see him also, running right toward her. But something wasn't quite right. He sensed she did not know who he was. She doesn't know it's me, he thought. The faster I run, the sooner she will see me. At the pace she was moving, they would run smack-dab into each other.

With sheer, precise abandon, he had seen his sister run like this. She was in a zone, and nothing would stop her from escaping that long, dark hole.

Thud! Aghh! Micah screamed. He slammed into Malia, but her left arm flung out intuitively and caught hold of him. He saw the relief in her eyes as she swept him up, steadied him, and swiftly turned him in the same direction she was running. They picked up their speed and didn't stop.

He ran faster to keep up his momentum. They ran like a house was on fire. Okay, he had to be honest with himself; Malia was running while holding onto him because his feet barely touched the ground. He needed to keep his reality in check.

Wretched cries began to reverberate evilness throughout the hollow chamber. Malia steadily propelled them both forward to the pinhole light, but the end of the tunnel remained at the same distance, never moving closer. The wailing cries came from all directions, trying to confuse the twins. Racing at top speed, Malia shouted, "This tunnel does not have an end! We must slow down and rest for a minute!"

Malia was still in motion as she slowly loosened her hold on Micah. He felt his body slide down, dragging his feet on the ground to a stop. Malia's grasp let go.

She stopped and turned in the opposite direction, but instead of running, she walked back toward the place they had tried to escape. She kept a laser focus on the dark tunnel walls behind them. Micah stood and watched her.

"We cannot completely stop, come on, we must keep moving." Malia grabbed her brother's arm just above the elbow and pulled him along. They walked side by side.

"You know, we Black people don't play this game. We don't believe in playing around with ghosts and demons. We run first and ask questions after." Malia was determined.

"That's for sure! I'm trying to figure out how we got here?" Micah coughed, his mouth dry and his throat scratchy.

"I do not have a clue, but we have to get out of here soon," she said.

"Did you see the thing, the monster?" Micah was in sheer terror.

"Yeah, I did. I don't know what it is, but it's not nice," Malia agreed.

Micah terrorized. "We must outthink the thing so that we can get home. It's all too crazy for me. I'm sorry. I don't get it."

"I can see them," Malia whispered, "but I don't understand what it is."

"What do you mean, them? I only saw one."

Malia looked at her brother. He trembled in the cold.

He knew what she was thinking. "I'm okay," he said, but his teeth chattered. It was dark and cold in there. He couldn't see in front of him.

"I wasn't ready to fight the creatures, but if I must, I will. I don't want to disappoint Papa." Malia's strong will and determination would please her grandfather.

Micah remembered what Papa said, "Fake it until you make it. You have everything you need inside of you."

"I'll make them afraid of me," Malia announced with all her bravado.

Micah knew she was brave, but this was a new twist. It was as if she had morphed into someone else. He realized this was just the beginning of the Dream Jumping journey.

Out of nowhere, two things begin to hover ten feet above them. They were formless things. Malia stood defiantly and pushed her brother behind her, but he stubbornly returned to her side.

The twins see the Wrathtors for the first time.
Illustration and Photography by Adrienne La Faye © 2022

"Will you stop acting like you're my savior? I can handle myself."
Although it was dark, he could see things.

She nodded and waited. Now they stood back-to-back. Micah's body shivered hard from the cold and fright, and the muscles in his arms and legs tightened.

He gasped for air, while Malia took her stand against these things. She placed her hands on her slim hips and firmly planted her legs into a wide stance. She was determined not to show her fear.

The demons started to hiss, crying out their threats. The things dared to circle above them, weaving in between the others, screeching high-pitched cries, leaving smoky black and red trails that dissipated in the atmosphere around them.

"Maaliiia and Micaaah, we are warning you now... do not go to the Dream Jumpers Academy. When you are asked to go, you must say NO."

One of the things moved even closer to them. The twins leaned backward to keep a safer distance from them. "If you go to the Academy, we will stop you at all costs, and you will be sorry. You think we are scary now— wait and see what you are up against."

Abruptly, the dream ended. The twins were safe and warm tucked back into their beds. They each lay very still in the silence, like stick men, blinking at the ceiling.

The following day, out of sheer terror, neither child dared to mention the nightmare.

CHAPTER SIX

WAITING FOR PAPA'S RETURN

"Not being able to talk about our gift is bothering me. Micah?" Malia sat on his bed. "Aren't you listening to me?"

"Will you stop talking? Hold on, and I must finish this before Papa gets here." Micah pointed his pen to the first line on his notepad, tapped up and down, then stopped and rested the pen on the desk. He turned to his computer and scrolled down the monitor, the text flashing through sections about the sixth sense.

"Can you at least tell me what you are researching?"

"Well, I'm looking for unexplainable supernatural visions and occurrences to see if I can make sense of what we've experienced. Unfortunately, there is too much for me to explain, but I will later."

Malia lay down halfway on the bed and squirmed around, observing her right foot as she swung it along the side of the bed. She wondered, how could we keep quiet and not tell anyone about this?

Her leg stopped, and she saw TJ facing the closet door. She thought he had been waiting too.

Finally, Papa materialized. How could he possibly know what was going on? Malia took TJ's lead, jumped up, and said it was time to go to the closet. They crawled into the vault one by one and waited just as Micah's watch alarm beeped. Papa appeared in the same tiny chair quicker than he had during his first visit.

Papa cupped his hands over his mouth like a bullhorn and tilted his head backward. The room shifted again, and the twins stared in amazement. Finally, Papa stood and shouted, "ARE YOU READY?"

They knew that drill. The older man would do this to get the kids pumped up and excited.

"Yes, we are!" The twins often said things in unison without meaning to do it. He shouted louder. "IT DOESN'T SOUND LIKE IT!" He bellowed. "ARE YOU READY?"

Malia stood up perfectly straight, just like her grandfather, and cleared her throat. Micah stayed seated with his hands firmly planted on his thighs and both legs stretched out. He had his ankles crossed in front of him and thought deeply about what his research revealed.

Papa stared down at him, but Micah looked at him with uncertainty. Then, unflinching, he probed his grandfather with questions.

"Papa, how are we just supposed to accept everything you tell us? I've done some research, and I haven't found anything to prove you're telling us the truth."

"Boy, if you don't get up and trust me—have I ever let you down the wrong path?"

"No, but I need more information before I accept...."

"Micah, we have to trust Papa. He knows what's best for us." Malia said with encouragement. She knew he hated surprises.

He reluctantly stands up, and Papa starts the mantra again. This time they all hollered from the top of their lungs.

"YES, WE ARE!" Continuously chanting five more times. "YES, WE ARE!"

Papa was finally convinced they were ready. "Okay, let's do this, then! Y'all, better get ready. We're going to school."

Malia's mouth fell open. She took several steps backward. "Whoa! NO. NO." She stood her ground, noticing that she was getting better at that.

"Don't you realize that we are on summer break? We are not going to be home-schooled on our vacation." She plopped down onto the child's chair, feeling the blow beneath her. She repeated under her breath, "No, No."

Micah shook his head and mumbled, "I am not going to school during the summer." He pouted his lips and defiantly folded his arms across his chest. "I knew you weren't telling us every-thing. We don't know what's happening, but you expect us to follow you blindly. You got to give me more."

Papa laughed loudly. He bent over to look Micah directly in his eyes. "It is not what you think. You are going to love . . . The one and the only . . . Dream Jumper Academy of the World!"

"Whaaat, there's a school for Dream Jumping?" Micah did a stomping dance but stopped abruptly. He remembered the night-mare when the monsters warned them not to go to the Academy.

"Hold on, wait one minute. It is not what you think. Yes, there is a school, and every Dream Jumper must attend. No exceptions." Papa confirmed.

Malia sensed the older man could see they were not going for it, so he changed his tactics.

"Okay, y'all take a couple of deep breaths, then hear me out." He raised his head and shoulders simultaneously, then relaxed them.

"This school will teach you how to practice your gift, and you both must go. It's your legacy. End of the story." He did not give them a choice. "Great, Aunt Thelma and I both went to the Dream Jumpers Academy of the World."

"Aunt Thelma went to the school with you?" Malia asked.

She was about to continue her questions, but Micah interrupted. "Remember, they're fraternal twins, so if Papa is a Dream Jumper, she has to be one too."

"That's right, son." Papa agreed. "Look, y'all, someone has to teach you Jumping skills. Y'all do not know what they are or how to use them. The Academy will help you develop your gifts to their highest potential. They will teach you what you need to know, and you will learn with other kids like you. The teachers are fantastic. Each teacher has been where you are now. You will be taught about things that you never imagined existed."

"There are other kids like us who also have the gift?" Malia questioned. The idea of kids that are like her and Micah made her exhale with relief. She thought about how great it would feel to fit in and not be the weird ones.

"Yes," said Papa. "The Academy will open your minds to this whole new world."

"Hello... Ah, what are we going to tell Father?" Micah scrutinizes the whole plan his grandfather concocted. Micah used his logic.

"Right, I need to mention something else. In the new world, time is calculated differently than you have been taught. Micah, you are the scientist and the mathematician. You will find time easy to grasp. Just use your brain. Time-Space Continuum is paradoxically calculated. One hour here in this world is equal to one month in the Jumper world." Papa adjusted his position to settle in and explain their new time spaces.

"Here's the best way to understand this time-space thing. You can be in two places at one time. The other world is so much faster. It is there you can do whatever you want and come back home to exist in this world, as though you never left." Papa was satisfied with his explanation. "Now, you should get it," Papa said. "Any more questions?"

The twins shook their heads slowly. "No."

Malia loved her Papa so much that she accepted what he said. "So, we can be gone for months or years in Jumper world and still be back in the morning—just like we never left?"

Their grandfather nodded in agreement. "I cannot promise that everything will be the same when you come back and wake up in the morning, but once you experience it, you will get the hang of it. As I said, I can show you better than I can tell you, so trust me."

His glorious smile suggested that their lives would improve as soon as they agreed.

Micah, smiling, said, "As long as we don't get in trouble and still get to have our summer vacation, I AM ALL IN!"

"That's the spirit. Let's get going. I have to get y'all there on time." Papa pompously dusted fake particles off his shoulder, sniffed the air, and then quoted himself, "As I say, the apple does not fall too far from the tree. Sometimes it rolls down the hill, but not in our family."

He bent over with laughter, holding his belly as if his sides hurt. "Before I forget, y'all did a fantastic job the other night in your dream."

Malia clutched her mouth and said, "How did you know about that?"

"It was real, and you did nothing to help us?" Micah was indignant.

"Y'all are on your own, and you have all that you need inside of you. The Academy will teach the rest." Papa nodded confidently. He ignored their bewilderment and grabbed one hand of each of the twins.

He inhaled until his lungs filled with air, then slowly discharged the breath through his rounded lips. His nostrils flared wide apart. Malia saw a gray nose hair flutter back and forth.

"Close your eyes," he demanded. "Imagine yourselves entering a higher realm."

The children complied. The transference state began.

A bugle horn blew. It announced their arrival into the new solar system.

"Papa?" Malia's eyes shut tight. "Can you explain what's happening right now?"

This was their welcome ceremony. In a nanosecond, the kids fell into a state of deep sleep. They felt their bodies clone, dividing into two of themselves. There were two of them now. The process was not scary at all. It felt like a normal. Their physical bodies stayed in the real world while an entirely new entity was created to exist in the other world.

Malia opened her eyes, blinked a few times, and watched their cloned bodies lift out of their real selves. Their earthly bodies would stay asleep while they were in their Dream Jumper bodies. Malia looked down at her body and then toward her brother. "Do I look okay?" Before Micah could ask her, she said, "You look great."

They all heard music playing in the distance. One soothing piano tinkled its keys, and its music notes appeared before them, so large it took up the entire space and lit the sky.

The warm new world they entered was filled with fantastical colors that flew toward them and around them. Malia was mesmerized by the vibrant colors that swirled around her. There were bright reds, blues, purples, greens, and oranges of various hues. It was a rainbow musical that multiplied into an abundance of possibilities!

It was an opulent and grand show. The enormous intensity affected the twin's emotions in a soothing, suddenly—waves of warm air blasted by them, catapulting them upward.

Malia began crying. She thought they had gone to heaven. She glanced over at her twin. He, too, had tears falling from his eyes. She felt a stronger pull, and their bodies ascended even higher into this new space. Papa turned back and waved for them to follow. The suction of upward gravity made it hard to hold their arms straight and legs together. Their limbs floated in the air about them.

Micah looked like the plastic blow-up man at a used car lot. His skinny body flailed about, back and forth and sideways, up and down. But, at least, the atmospheric force field kept him elevated in the air. Otherwise, he would have tumbled down.

"Hey, son," said Papa, "don't worry. You are doing a good job. This is your first time." Micah relaxed and felt reassured by those words.

His sister's body was coordinated, as usual, hands held by her sides and her feet and legs in perfect alignment. Papa gave her a nod, proud of her flying skills. Malia enjoyed the ride, and it felt natural. She proved a skilled flyer, but she tried to clear her mind of it so she would not get a big head.

A gust of wind suddenly came from below, propelling them left and right.

Then the descent to the school began. They converged onto a vast woodland area landscaped with trees, shrubs, and flowers of every color and variety that no one in the real world could ever imagine.

Malia saw her brother off to the right. He was still having trouble with his balance. He had missed a lot of the transformation because he struggled the whole time. She wanted to laugh so badly but knew this was not the place or the time to tease him.

Next, she spotted a glimpse of a building that might be the Academy. Lush green trees enveloped the building on an island surrounded by water and sandy beaches. Jagged rocks outlined small foothills that gradually increased into more massive hills that formed cliffs that lined the shores so high they disappeared into the clouds. All one could see beyond the cliffs were miles of royal blue water.

Malia and Micah got to school.
Illustration and Photography by Adrienne La Faye ©
2022

Their descent continued while the morning sky turned into a swirl of pink and orange clouds. They descended closer to the new world and saw children standing in twelve single rows: six lines of girls and six lines of boys

The children were being herded into their proper paths. Micah and Malia touched softly down on the ground, like feathers, without feeling shaky or disoriented.

Papa cleared his throat. "Micah, I expect you to use your brains and take care of your sister."

Malia and Micah were one pair of new Jumpers at the Academy. They looked at each other and agreed they were ready for their new lessons in this new world. Malia was momentarily frightened as they approached the school, but the feeling dissipated in an instant.

CHAPTER
SEVEN

CUBE ASSIGNMENT

"Your names, please?" An older pinched-faced white girl stood at the entrance of the school, directing the newcomers to their correct lanes.

"I'm Malia, and 'here's my brother, Micah."

"Get in line, and your orientation counselors will take you to your next phase. Malia, your counselor, has gone to welcome the next pair of new students."

The twins looked at a school made entirely from mirrored glass, which reflected the forest, which in turn caused the school disappears into the foliage. Micah could see in through the school's opened doors, but he could not see through the darkened mirrored windows.

The building looked brand new to him, and everything seemed technologically state of the art. There were various doors leading straight up or straight down a hall and doors leading high up on the walls—and some doors were built down onto the floors.

The lobby was massive. Micah thought the thick glass double doors had to be bulletproof. The floor moved, detached, and separated into 25-inch by 25-inch squares. Color-coded squares lit up when the children stood on them. Each companion square was set in single file on a moving sidewalk. There were six lines for girls and six lines for boys. In each line, there were twelve new Jumpers. When the Jumpers entered the Academy for the first time, they were assigned one color-coded square and instructed to stand on it. A handrail was provided for support.

When his blue square lit up, Malia saw her brother's eyes fill with joy. Micah was still clumsy in his growing body, and one of his big ole' size sixteens slipped off his foot. The shoe flopped up and would have fallen to the floor below if there weren't a handrail to brace himself. He tried to play it off as though it was no big deal, like he was surveying the school's surroundings or something.

Malia pointed down at her orange companion square. "These are sweet." She was also unaware of its function, but she liked how the orange color glowed beneath her and cast a warm hue onto her medium-brown skin.

Micah gave her a thumb's up. He could not wait to figure out how they worked.

All the children took their places on their squares and waited in anticipation for what would happen next. They all had a wide-eyed look of bewilderment as they watched the magic around them.

The furniture in the lobby transformed into different configurations right before their eyes. Micah watched a kid stand up from a chair to leave, and the chair collapsed and dropped to the floor.

Then, he realized that the only part that moved was the walking sidewalk and squares for the new enrollees.

Micah could tell that Malia would fit in right away. She was more adventurous. Micah let out a sigh of exasperation. He had no idea what would happen next, and he did not like surprises, which was why he had so many notepads. He had a quest for knowledge and researched all sorts of his thoughts and subjects.

The companion squares began to move forward, but unlike a moving sidewalk in the real world, the squares detached and separated the twins: all girls glided to the left, and all boys glided to the right.

The new Jumpers were startled by the sudden movement of the squares and grasped their handrails tightly to steady their balance. The children screamed in delight and surprise at this sleek new ride they were standing on.

Micah kept his sister in sight until she disappeared; he assumed she would meet her counselor. He hated change without being prepared. Micah checked out every boy that passed by and tried to read their expressions to see if they enjoyed the environment. So far, he was not enjoying it.

Fear of the unknown took hold of him. He began to sweat and tried to remember where he entered the building so he could make a clean getaway.

The children were greeted by their Academy counselors and whisked into rooms, either on the left or right. When Micah thought no counselor would claim him, the line stopped, and to his right stood a noticeably short man. He was a little Caucasian person.

He looked up at Micah. "Hello, Mr. Oliver. I am your orientation counselor, Mr. Little. Follow me so I can get you checked in. I will assign you a cube you will share with other Jumpers, then you and your classmates will go to dinner."

Micah wanted to ask Mr. Little how he knew his name but thought the counselor had the gift of mind-reading. He answered Micah's thought. "It's my job to know every child under my care.

I do have the gift of knowing. And, besides, I saw a photo of you and read your file."

The man let out a chuckle. He then turned, slightly dragging his foot, and walked into his office. Micah still gripped the handrail of his square as it glided behind the man.

He noticed that Mr. Little's right leg was shorter than his left. His foot was deformed compared to the right one.

"Don't worry, you are going to fit in here," Mr. Little said, following up to reassure the new student as he sat in his chair behind his desk. "You will finally get to be with your peers who also have gifts.

One of the benefits of attending Dream Jumpers, The Academy, is that you will find the answers to questions you have had your entire life but were too afraid to ask. Remember all of those unexplained visions?"

Mr. Little picked up a clipboard and pen from his desk. He instructed the bewildered and frightened boy to step off his square and sit in the chair across from him.

Micah analyzed every inch of the man's face. Micah's elbows pressed onto the chair's-stained armrests. He wanted to ask essential questions but did not know what to ask. Instead, he glanced around the room, looking for a subject.

He then pointed to a plaque on the wall surrounded by photos of children from around the world with the inscription: "Successful Jumper Graduates."

"Do you know all those kids in the pictures, Mr. Little?"

"Yes, I do," he answered gently. "These are all the children I have counseled." He glanced down at the clipboard, on the tip of his nose, at a set of black, thick-rimmed reading glasses. "Okay, let's get started. What is your full name?

"I am Micah Brandon Oliver, "he responded with pride, as Papa had taught him.

"What is your age?"

"I am twelve, but I'll be thirteen next month." When you are about to be another age soon, it's important to clarify that, he thought. "I have a question."

The man raised his eyes from the clipboard and peered over his black glasses before answering.

He replied coolly, "Yes?"

"Sir, why are you asking me questions when you know the answers? Why not just read my mind?"

The counselor kept his gaze on the boy. Then a light went on in Micah's head. "Oh! I know why. You know what I'm thinking, but I don't know what you're thinking."

"It is a precautionary measure. Although I have never been wrong during my twenty-eight years in service as an orientation counselor, it is better to be safe than sorry."

The boy thought about this man and discerned he was a close-up person, not liking to say too much. In amusement, Mr. Little shook his head, knowing what the boy was thinking. What Micah reckoned that gesture was to unload cobwebs of memories.

He stood from his chair and handed Micah a blue drawstring bag filled with all these items. "Don't worry. You are supplied with all the standard necessities and more." Micah took the thick bundle and placed it on his lap.

Mr. Little explained to Micah the function of the squares. "Now, you will have many questions, and that is why we assign everyone a companion square. You can ask the companion square questions at any time. You will be here for a while, so prepare to hunker down because you can't leave until you graduate."

Unbelievable! It was too late. They got him. He was stuck here. It never dawned on Micah to ask his grandfather if they could leave the Academy if they wanted to. His mind raced.

He could not believe that Papa would trick him into giving up his summer vacation without letting him prepare for all of this.

Micah's eyes darted to the door of the room. He devised an escape plan as he retrieved his trusted notepad from his pants pocket.

Mr. Little glanced at the boy and casually said, "You can leave any time you want, but there's no returning once the doors close behind you." Micah's escape plan must have appeared like a diagram smack dab in the middle of his worry wrinkled forehead.

Micah needed options. He wanted the choice to leave if he did not fit in with the other kids. Everything happened too quickly for him. He was not prepared for all this new stuff.

He needed more information and time, but his reality quickly sank in, and he remembered that the man across from him could read his mind. The corners of his mouth turned up slightly. He smiled at him sheepishly.

Micah held his class uniforms and necessities close to his chest with his left arm and stepped onto his square. He grasped the handrail with his right. Mr. Little escorted him out of the room and to his new cube.

CHAPTER
EIGHT

FALLING FROM
GRACE

The boys in Micah's cube watched him from their beds, waiting for the counselor to leave. Micah said goodbye to Mr. Little.

"Hey, dude, what's your name?" A robust athletic-built kid spoke.

"I am Micah." He set his drawstring bundle on his bed and began to unpack.

The athletic kid pointed to the short, massive boy sitting on the bed across from him. "This is Moon Washington, and I am Jackson Phillips. Where are you from?"

Micah stared at both boys as they waited for him to reply. "I am from Seattle. Well, my sister and I are from there."

He hung up his uniforms in an empty closet and realized his new roommates were watching him with uncertainty, but he stayed quiet. Jackson took Micah's silence as an invitation to move closer to him.

"Dude, can I count on you to do my homework?"

"Why would I want to help you?" Micah was incredulous. "I haven't even unpacked yet. Besides, that would be cheating.

Jackson replied, "Dude, I can tell by looking at you. You love school. You just have that study type look." Jackson took a step backward. "Man, stop tripping, it's okay. I was just asking."

"Jackson, don't worry about him," Moon chimed in. "I can help you . . ."

"Dang, your feet are gigantic!" Jackson exclaimed. "What size shoes do you wear?"

"Sixteen."

"I hope you grow fast because you walk like Ronald McDonald. Blah ha!"

Micah could hear his father look him in the face and tell him to shut the hell up.

Jackson changed the subject and asked, "Hey, man, do you know where our sisters are?" Jackson closed in on Micah, too close for his comfort, so he stepped back and mumbled, "No, dude, I don't."

He turned his back to the boys and moved toward the wall to design his section of the cube. He wasn't used to being around kids, except for Malia, and she didn't count. He hadn't talked to another kid in a long time and felt claustrophobic. There was so much that he hadn't had the chance to process, like talking to other kids. How was he going to do that?

They were homeschooled to avoid the questions of Malia's super strength and his super-intellect, and they think very differently than most children their age. The most obvious reason he thinks SO THEY WON'T EMBARRASS THEIR FATHER.

Jackson kept the conversation going and added. "I am from Dallas."

"I'm from Detroit," Moon mimicked Jackson.

Micah looked over his shoulder. It was his turn to say something.

"How . . . How long have you guys been here?" He quickly turned his back to them. He isn't interested in small talk.

"We got here today," Jackson answered for both boys. Clearly, the kid wasn't too smart, Micah thought. Of course, they'd all arrived today because it was the first day of the Academy. Sheesh!

He meant how long they had been in the room. He tried reading the boys' thoughts but got nothing.

Jackson's skin was the color of a milk chocolate bar. The Dude was taller than most kids he'd seen around their neighborhood and very athletically built.

He may have been held back a couple of grades because he was too big to be the same age. That boy had confidence. He had swagger.

By contrast, Moon was a short, plump light-skinned Asian teen with a face that spelled out he was a worrier. His eyebrows knitted together in a unibrow, and his buckteeth wore braces.

He used a wide belt to hold his pants high up on his waist, which made it difficult to look at him.

Micah felt that Moon was trying desperately to fit in with Jackson. To escape these dudes, he checked out the bathroom since he was the last to arrive.

The boy needed to write down a few things first. He sat at his desk, arranged his belongings, and updated his notepad.

"So, fellas, let's ride our companions. Hey, Dude, ya coming?" Jackson asked. No one moved. The big guy sat on the edge of his bed and cracked his knuckles while trying to think of something else to do.

Micah ignored him. He wrote his thoughts on his notepad. Charting the information down could see the big picture. He needed to have ready solutions to the problems that he and his sister might encounter to be ahead of the game. He turned on his desk lamp and wiggled in his chair to get more comfortable.

1. **Soundproof doors.**
2. **No visible door locks.**
3. **There are a lot of kids everywhere.**
4. **Companion squares are both individual computers and transportation.**

A few minutes passed, and Moon clapped his hands together. "Hey, I got it! Are y'all hungry? I have to be honest; I need to eat."

This time Jackson jumped up. "I'm going to ride my companion square first. In a minute, yeah, sure, we can go to the cafeteria. I'm not sticking around this dump."

Micah grunted without looking at either kid. "Y'all go ahead. I will catch up with you later. I have work to do."

Jackson shrugged his shoulders, feeling confident about his new ride, and made a full stride toward the door. Out of his periphery,

Micah saw that Moon was watching his massive move and tried to walk smoothly like Jackson, but his pants made a swish sound as his thighs rubbed tightly against each other.

"Dude, what is that sound coming from your pants?" Moon stopped in his tracks. "I don't hear anything."

Jackson said, "Man, it's alright. I know it's your pants, and you're just big-boned."

Micah turned to watch him laugh at the boy without any guilt.

Moon laughed too like he didn't care, and Micah thought, if he doesn't care, why should I?

He turned again to see what Jackson was laughing at now. Moon was trying to copy the cool boy by pulling his belt even tighter to further restrict the movement of his pants. It must have bored Jackson because he had left the room. Moon stayed in the doorway to watch Jackson step onto his square.

Micah watched out of the corner of his eye and wanted to know what the boys were doing. Moon's eyes shone brightly. He slapped one hand to his forehead and shouted, "That is incredible! This guy is awesome. Did you just see that?"

Micah heard some kids cheering on Jackson and clapping their hands. He jumped up to watch the athlete swagger on his square. He stood triumphantly with hands on his waist as he pumped out his chest, just like Superman. Jackson's stance on his square looks effortless. He glided past his cube, making airplane wings with his arms. Show off.

Jackson now bent in a squat position. He stretched his left leg straight out in front of him and extended his arms out to his sides. He did airplane maneuvers as he wove in and out, up and down, and spun out, making airplane noises as he flew around.

Micah placed a hand on the left side of his chest. He felt his heart racing. His index and middle finger are on his wrist to count his pulse. He wanted to throw up.

He was way too awkward to compete with the likes of Jackson. So how did the guy do that?

Jackson landed with ease. "Man, I am just getting started. Wait and see what I do next time. Come on, Moon, it is your turn."

Moon stood on his square cautiously. He balanced himself, then shifted his weight, and off he went about twenty feet from the floor.

He turned his square back around and landed. The whole time his mouth was wide open, his unibrow somehow made its way up to the edge of his hairline. He cautiously stepped off his square, puffing hard as if he had just run a marathon.

"Okay, Micah! You're up! Show us whatcha working with."

Micah thought I could handle this, so he took his turn. He firmly planted one foot on the companion and let the other dangle off.

He extended both arms to the side, trying to gain his balance. He managed a smile to the fellas watching below, but there was sheer fear behind it.

From the get-go, it was too much, and he knew it. When he tried to stand up, his shoes were too heavy, and he lost his balance. He fell. He screamed as he plummeted to the ground. All kinds of students came out of the woodwork, running to see what was happening.

They saw a boy high above them, falling from the ceiling. "Help me, help me!" No one moved because no one knew what to do. Then, out of nowhere, his companion square shot down past him and grew wider.

The backside of his body met the square, which quickly adjusted for his weight, and he dropped another foot. He laid spread eagle on the square. The sides grew up three feet to keep him from falling off.

His square went in a circle and gained altitude above the assembled groups of kids. Micah thought the whole Academy was now standing on their balconies watching this catastrophe.

Instead, thee square whisked him to the door of his cube. Some kids said they are glad he didn't get hurt, while others said he is a klutz. And his roommates.

Well, they are not that generous. He sat on his square on the floor in front of his cube, motionless and utterly humiliated.

Jackson and Moon laughed hard, mocking him. Micah crawled off his companion, his feet slapping as he did the walk of shame into his cube. He tried to keep his composure, but his hands shook as he picked his notepad out of his pants pocket:

Make time to learn how to ride that thing.

I will master this.

Moon shouted, "Man, you suck!" He looked at Jackson to join in the mockery, and Jackson took the bait.

"Seriously, Dude, you almost died! Next time use your feet like their brakes to stop you! They're big enough! HA! HA! HA!"

Moon added to the ridicule. "You walk like a slab of cement is attached to your feet. They're so big they have a mind of their own." "You're not going to make it here, dude." Jackson pointed to

Micah's massive feet and bent over with laughter.

Moon walked next to Jackson to separate himself from Micah. "I bet you can't ride a tricycle without getting your toes stuck under the wheel!"

The two boys laughed and chortled. Jackson mimicked him by standing on one foot and holding out the other, as if he was falling, and flailing his arms around in the air. "Uh Ohhh...!"

Micah had never been in this situation, so he didn't know what to do. He sat on his bed and ignored them as much as possible.

Then, keeping his back to the boys and tightly gripped his fist until his hand became weak. Then, inhaling and exhaling, seeking calmness, he scratched on his pad: Nothing had changed. I'm still as clumsy. How do I fix this?

He squeezed his eyes shut, and an image of Papa came into focus. Papa waved, and he heard him say, "Boy, don't you worry about them fools. You have everything you need inside you." He opened one eye at a time and looked around to see if the idiots had seen his vision too.

He didn't know if they had the gift to see what he saw. No, they were out of the room.

"Thanks, Papa." He felt lighter emotionally, but he would never forget this. He held his head high. I have everything that I need inside me. "Micah, Micah." Micah heard his name being called by his sister "Jackkkson," he heard. "Jaaaack."

Their twin sisters found them in their cube, surprising them with their flying abilities. Malia was the first to fly her square up and land. Jackson and Moon's sisters flew in much slower. Once they were all together, they introduced themselves.

Micah thought each of the twins looked alike. The twins were fraternal but had strong resemblances.

"We were just on our way to find you all," announced Moon. Brianna is Jackson's sister, and she asked, "Where should we go?" "Let's get a snack," said Moon. "We're hungry."

Moon's sister was aptly named Star. She was tubby like her brother. "Follow me," she said. "The cafeteria is keyed in as number one on my square."

Micah was so glad to see his sister. She knew immediately that something was wrong with him. She gave him a wink and gently elbowed his arm to lift his spirits.

He understood and pretended he had gotten himself together.

Together, the three sets of twins flew to the cafeteria.

"Sis, hold on a minute," he said, holding her forearm. "Let those guys go ahead, okay?"

Malia noticed some kids pointing at Micah as they passed by on their squares. Some kids avoided passing by him and waited for the two to pass by. "Let's wait," one girl said to her twin. "He might knock us off. Let him go ahead."

At that moment, Mr. Little rode up to them and asked, "Micah, are you okay? I heard you fell off your square. Do you need me to do anything? I think you should have a doctor look you over."

Most of the others gave them ample room to fly by, but only Moon and Jackson snickered and smiled.

"What happened?" Malia asked, "I'll make them pay." "I'll tell you in a minute."

Micah lifted his arm and gave Mr. Little the signal to stop. "Thanks, Mr. Little, I'm good. I didn't fall—the companion came and swooped me up and took me to my room. Can you . . . Like. . . not make a bigger deal than it already is?"

Mr. Little understood and knew that the whole school was talking about him. "Remember, I'm here to help you any time you need me." He skittered away.

Micah saw that his sister was clearly shaken, but he was not going to let anything stop him from becoming an excellent Dream Jumper.

"Micah," she said, "Don't worry. We're going to be the best Jumping team ever!"

CHAPTER
NINE

NO REDEMPTION
FRIENDS

Jackson and the boys continued to laugh at Micah for his major blunder on his companion square. In retaliation to the taunts and teasing, Micah did not say a word.

Micah and Malia decided to hang out with a set of twins who arrived late at the Academy. Tanisha and her twin brother, Mondarius, explained to them why they were late. Micah asked all the questions because he was suspicious of them. Micah was suspicious of everyone since he had no friends.

Mondarius explained that it all started with their grandmother, who they call, Granny, who had passed away. He kept hearing a voice that sounded like hers who told him that she was their Granny. They would get scared and run away to escape the voice and ignore its calls out to them.

He continued to explain that he and Tanisha grew up in a big city with many scammers, so they were not buying easily into it.

Tanisha and Mondarius tell their story, but it is mostly Mondarius who monopolizes the conversation. He animated his account using his hands in grand gestures and made funny faces for his biggest laugh. He had Malia and Micah laughing hysterically about everything he and his sister did to keep the voice from getting too close to them.

Mondarius laughed too and was unaware of the little snort he gave out as he continued, which made the children laugh even harder. He could barely tell his story without laughing. "Yo . . . We even made doubles of ourselves with our clothes, hats, sunglasses, and shoes. You name it; we would use it."

The children were uproarious. Malia loved their story, it was like their story, but the way Mondarius told his story was much funnier. "Micah, doesn't this sound like us?" He nodded his head because he enjoyed listening to this fast-talking kid's story, and he hung onto his every word.

Mondarius knew how to tell a story. He reminded the children of a stand-up comedian. The pitch of his voice gradually rose at all the funny parts. He used his whole body to tell his story, moving his arms back and forth when he talked about running away and making his eyes wide as saucers at the scary stuff.

Mondarius had the children's attention, so kept it going. "Then we'd put the dummies in our beds and on chairs all around the house, day and night." He covered his mouth with his hand and giggled. "We were too scared to go to bed. So, we'd hide in the closet and wait all night to see if THE THING would show itself."

Malia looked at Micah, thinking they had a closet story, too, but it didn't sound as funny as this one.

"We were ready to beat the crap out of it." Mondarius threw a punch in the air. "We had bats, a nail gun, nails, darts, pretty much anything to defend ourselves. But it didn't matter what we had because we couldn't stay awake long enough to see anything." Mondarius chuckled and shook his head.

"Y'all should've set your alarm to wake you up," said Micah.

"Thanks, bro, but it's too late for that," Mondarius gave him a wide-eyed, goofy expression, and the children all laughed.

"Yea, you're right! Keep going."

"Now, we didn't know about this Academy, so this morning the old lady knew she had to step up her game to convince us she was our Granny and get us here on time." The twins were silent, waiting for Mondarius's next punch line.

"So, this morning, we're eating breakfast and watching TV, and out of nowhere, Granny was on the TV! I'm mean, she was actually inside the TV talking to us." He clutched his head in disbelief. Again, the pitch of his voice kicked up a note, still amazed by this supernatural anomaly.

Mondarius was a wisecracker, "She had that tone adults use when they ain't playing anymore, and you better listen up." They all nodded in agreement. They knew that tone.

Malia realized this guy was a great storyteller, and by the look in Micah's eyes, he was cool with their new friends.

"We were stuck-like-chuck and couldn't say a word. "Then, using his best Granny voice, he says, "If y'all play one more trick on me, I'm going to booby trap this whole house and haunt it forever. Y'all ain't never gone ever get a peaceful night's sleep, especially in that pitiful closet you call a hiding place."

"Maaan . . . She got our attention." Mondarius's eyes were so wide-open the twins thought they might be stuck in his head. "We were like, say what? Did she say she's going to haunt us even more?"

"Man, she was definitely a ghost." Tanisha finally chimed into the storytelling.

Malia thought to herself, thank God Tanisha found her voice. "Yes, ma'am," said the girl, "we're listening."

"We're sit-in' there trembling, almost sobbing, hoping, and praying for the ghost to leave. But noooooo, Granny didn't go." He paused briefly to build anticipation. "Can you guess what she did next?" Mondarius slid a little closer to the twins and paused his story just long enough to hit his punch line. Malia shook her head. Micah said nothing, too afraid of what was coming next.

Mondarius looked straight into the eyes of the twins. "She stepped right out of the TV, in the flesh-and-blood! She walked up to us and said, 'look me straight in the eyes. Now, when Granny tells you to do something—you do it."

Mondarius switched back to his Granny voice. "Now look at me and tell me that I'm not your Granny." He paused for just a moment, swallowed, and with utter disbelief, he said, "Then she hugged us!" He lowered his head as his eyes filled and gazed toward the floor.

"Right then, we both started bawling like there was no tomorrow. We realized the voice was our Granny." Mondarius slowed down the speed of his narration as he ended his story and somberly said, "It was cool, you know, to have her like . . . Be there . . . for real, because we missed her. She was the only one who loved us." Tanisha had a half-smile because her lips began to quiver, and tears filled her eyes as she listened to her brother's account of the story.

"We had been so hard-headed by the time she explained everything to us, and we were already late for school. She didn't care. She was set on getting us here, no matter how late."

Micah was still suspicious of Mondarius, even though he enjoyed his story. He never met anyone like those him. What did they want from Malia and him?

CHAPTER
TEN

CAFETERIA
FIGHTING
CHALLENGE

The cafeteria was gigantic. The room was lined with every vending machine the children would ever need, from ceiling to floor, and reached up beyond the children's view. The Jumpers left their companion squares outside the cafeteria and walked into the room, mesmerized by what they saw around them. Upon closer inspection, Micah counted twenty mirrors across the room, multiplying the reflections of the vending machines and bouncing light across the room in diagonal directions.

Three sets of twins entered the cafeteria at the same time: Moon and his sister Star, Jackson and his sister Brianna, and Malia and Micah.

They smelled homemade food being prepared as they entered the room, and for Moon, it seemed like a five-star restaurant.

"Wait a minute, do we need money?" asked Micah, being the sensible one.

"Dude, we don't need any money here." Moon was keyed up. "We can have all the food we want for free! I read it in the orientation booklet."

The children browsed the room, taking in the sights and delicious smells. Micah stumbled over his big feet as he inspected the vending machines. The children gave a brief chuckle, and this opened a new opportunity for Jackson, Moon, and some of the other boys to poke fun at him.

Jackson continued to taunt Micah for his clumsiness, the size of his feet, and his ludicrous fall off his companion square. Micah refused to give in to the heckling, and he remained silent. No matter how bad it got, he was not going to fight.

Malia, however, did have a lot to say. She was fed up with the bullying her brother was receiving from these dumb fools. But she knew she had her gift strength to back her up, hearing Papa's words in her head; everything you need is inside you.

Malia walked directly up to Jackson and pointed her finger at his face. Then, she shouted, "You need to get a life, bro, and get off my brother's back! He almost died today! Why don't you try that crap with me right now since you're acting like a super-duper Jumper!"

Jackson was arrogant with her. "Thank you for noticing that I am a super-duper Jumper. Don't be upset at me because you ain't as good as I am." He laughed directly in her face.

Malia was furious but scared too. She had never challenged anyone in her life, but she was irate with Jackson. Malia could feel something inside her change. Her character and courage shifted and became more assertive, more dominant—as though it wasn't her.

Micah didn't have a chance to make it at the Academy if he didn't fit in with the others, but at least she could help defend him. Micah shied away from confrontation or argument.

He was the most intelligent person she knew, but he could not stand up for himself.

Jackson was outraged. He turned around, looking at all corners of the cafeteria to see who witnessed this mouse of a girl challenging him. Malia's stare was piercing, and as she stared him down, she became acutely aware of his thick athletic frame.

He was big, and she assumed no one had ever challenged him because the look of surprise on his face was hilarious. He glared down at her, but Malia was resolute to see this through to the end, no matter the outcome. *What am I doing? Who am I becoming?*

Malia moved in closer, pointing her finger within an inch of his face. "I don't know who you think you are, but I will not let you harass my brother." She stood him down. "Micah has not done one thing to you.

He is one of the nicest kids you will ever meet, and I will not let you make his life hell." Her hands were now on her hips, waiting for his rebuttal.

Jackson gave Micah a look and sneered. "Dudes, are you kidding me. You're going to let your sister, a gurl, defend you? You serious, man?"

Micah responded in a small voice, "I'm not afraid of you. It doesn't make sense to fight." His twin could not hear him, so he repeated himself a little louder, "Man, I not afraid of you, but I'm not going to fight you either!"

Malia and Jackson both ignored him.

"Dude, you're tripping. It doesn't matter that I'm a girl," she hollered. "When I get done with you, you'll be afraid to say my name!" Malia felt emboldened.

"Okay, gurl, come on since you asking to get beat up. Let's do this." Jackson threw the gauntlet. "Do you think I won't hit a gurl? I'll knock you clean out!"

His sister Brianna pulled on her brother's arm and said to him in a faint voice, "I know you can beat her. Everybody here knows you can beat her, but this is not the right time."

Jackson jerked his arm away from his sister, smiling and feeling even bolder as this face-off continued. "Come on, accept the challenge." His body language shifted, doing a boxer's side-to-side dance, pumping himself up for a fight.

There was an edge of nervousness coming out of him as his lips began to quiver. "Somebody better tell this gurl who I am because she's messed with the wrong guy."

The tubby Washington twins kept eating through this entire display of bravado, laughing like they were at a dinner theater show. Malia's temper shifted, too. She clapped her hands and slowly walked in a circle while checking around the cafeteria to see who was watching her. She wanted to make Jackson feel small. Malia spouted loud enough for everyone to hear, "Great speech for a bully! Come on, dude! Let's do this outside, so we'll have enough room to fly."

Both children stomped out of the cafeteria and stepped onto their squares that were kept just outside the cafeteria door.

Now, Malia knew she was a solid athlete and was confident enough to be as good or better than the boy. She had strength behind her and figured out how to maneuver her companion square. She was confident of winning this fight or at least making Jackson think twice about messing with her brother.

Micah managed to get his big ole' sloppy feet to move in concert with his body and followed Malia out into the hallway. "You can't do this. We agreed not to make ourselves targets.

Everyone is going to hate us now more than ever!"

Malia understood her brother. She blamed their father, who had beaten the fight out of him. That man would punk him every chance he got because he hated his son.

Malia winked at her twin and said, "I got this! We're not hiding or running from anyone eva, eva again! I'm tired of bullies. So, I am ending this right now."

It grew dark outside. The children had been at the Academy for only one day, and already there was a fight. The companion squares lit up just as Malia and Jackson flew out through the Academy's front double doors.

They drifted toward the back of the Academy building, where there was tall wheatgrass. She could smell the saltwater of the ocean around them. A hot breeze clung to her face.

Most of the kids from the cafeteria stepped on their squares and flew outside to watch the fight. Companion squares glowed like bright fireflies in the dark evening sky. Some of the boys began to chant, "Shut her up! Shut her up! Shut her up!"

Malia looked toward the gathering crowd and saw her new friend, Tanisha, flying directly at her. "Listen, are you sure you want to fight this idiot?"

"Yeah, I'm sure." Malia retorted, "I am not afraid of this fool." "You've made up your mind, right? No one can talk you out of this?" Tanisha was determined, too, to convince Malia not to fight this bigheaded bully.

Malia nodded, trying to figure out why she would help her. "I got your back, okay," Tanisha whispered. "I'll make sure he doesn't cheat, and if he does, I'll fly over and distract him, which will give you more time to figure out your next move. By the way, I know

you can beat him." Tanisha gave a confident smile and flew off to the side. She was smaller than Malia but not afraid to get involved.

The children all knew the one unspoken rule of fighting: Do not interfere in a fight unless one person pulls a dirty move.

In her peripheral vision, Malia saw her cube mates watching idly on their squares. The girls floated in the front of the crowd. They folded their arms, dismayed by Malia's behavior, and did not even ask her if she would be okay.

Jackson began the brawl. "I thought you wanted to fight! But, of course, you can concede right now and let the whole Academy know that I'm the best Jumper here!" He towered over Malia. "If you want to back out, this is your last chance. Admit it! Say out loud that Jackson is the best Jumper in the school, and I'll let you go without beating your butt!"

Malia looked for Micah. He was behind her, suspended in the air, and yelled to her, "You don't have to do this! Who cares what he thinks?"

She winked at him to let him know she was ready. She turned to face her opponent, sped directly to the boy, and punched him smack dab in the mouth. She did it so quickly that it dazed him, and he staggered off his square. His arms thrashed in the air to catch his square, and then he held on, dangling in the air until the square adjusted to his fall and lowered down to his waist.

He pulled himself up and laid across the square. He stumbled about to regain his balance, dazed by the blow to his face.

Sweet justice, Malia thought to herself. "Now YOU fell off your square! How does it feel? Did you pee your pant?"

The crowd laughed along with her and began to cheer her on. At that moment, she saw Micah looking up into the trees. Her stunning punch at Jackson must have terrified her brother because he flew away like he was dodging something.

She went hard for Jackson again, but this time he was ready for her. He swung at her head but missed. She taunted Jackson by circling him and daring him to fight harder. She knew she was too fast for this big shot. Jackson regrouped from the hit to the face and was in hot pursuit of her.

It was pitch black dark outside, and Malia could only see the lights from the squares, no faces; and was startled when someone shouted to her, "You can beat him!"

The boys began to chant again, "Kick her butt! Kick her butt!" Malia was caught off guard and gave a glance toward the boys. Jackson closed in, flew ahead of her, crisscrossed back, then flew straight to her and punched her square in the stomach.

The blow barely hurt her. Jackson paused to shake out the pain in his fist. He waited for her to come back at him. Then, finally, he began to realize that this girl was healthy.

Malia was ready to knock him off his square again. She darted toward him, grabbing him firmly around the waist. He caught her, too, and they wrestled on their squares that hovered in midair. Tanisha flew close to Malia, ready to help.

The fighting Jumpers took a swift nosedive, but they didn't notice they were headed straight toward the ground. But then, something more powerful took control of them. Malia and Jackson would not let go of their grasp on the other, and they quickly approached the rocks and the cliffs below.

She wouldn't be the first to let go. That would make her look weak and afraid, and she wasn't. She looked up behind Jackson to see Micah flying toward her. He shouted from the top of his lungs, "Malia, let him go! You're going to hit the rocks! Let him go, or you will die!"

Tanisha flew down to catch up with them. She had Malia's back. She'd promised her.

The sound of sheer terror in her brother's voice frightened her. She let go of Jackson. Her square pulled her up just in time as she grazed the top of the tall wheatgrass.

A siren rang out, like a battleship warning' hands-on-deck.' It startled the children, and they quieted down. The exterior intercom crackled on, and a robotic-sounding voice announced: All students must return to their cubes at once.

Counselors on their companions flew toward the crowd to herd the children back inside. Some of the older kids, who were the monitors for the new Jumpers, scooted their squares between Malia and Jackson to separate them.

Micah grabbed Malia by the hand and yanked her toward him. He shuttled her to a secluded area behind the building. "I thought you were going to hurt him, not commit suicide. Are you okay?"

She sat on her square, legs crossed, and looked over his shoulder. There was that Tanisha girl. She did have her back. Tanisha swooped up next to Malia and sat down on her square, too. "Dang, girl, you're fierce. I could tell from the way you control your square. You just needed more time with him, and you would've won."

"You could've gotten hurt?"

"Those types of guys will jump you if they think you're by yourself," Tanisha said. "I don't think that's right, so I was your wing woman." Malia studied her words and thanked her.

Mondarius flew up next to them. "Y'all, that was some crazy stuff. What did you do, gurl, to get into a fight on the first day of school?" Mondarius was stunned by what he had just seen. "How did this start, and why weren't we there to see it pop off?"

Micah interrupted the entire conversation. "Hey, we can talk later. Let's get inside before we all get in some serious trouble." The four children began their flight back to the Academy. Mondarius was silent, and then asked Micah, "Hey, man, what floor are you on?"

Micah ignored the boy, but Mondarius kept asking the question until Micah grumbled, "The fourth level." He turned his back to Mondarius, again not wanting to engage in small talk.

"Thanks for having my back, Tanisha." "It's cool, no big deal."

Tanisha and Mondarius scooted ahead and flew into the Academy.

Micah grabbed his sister's arm as they turned the corner, "We are in some serious trouble." The twins' counselors flew toward them, quickly shooing them back into the school.

Why aren't you inside gathering your belongings?" Ms. Topperhead said to Malia. She was terse with her.

"We're sorry. I didn't know we were supposed to," Malia apologized.

"The Chancellor announced twenty minutes ago that everyone was being reassigned to live with their sibling," said Mr. Little. "Move along and gather your things. We'll be around if you need us. Hurry up! Get your stuff."

"Mr. Little, are you kidding? We get to the room with our twin?" Micah perked up.

"Yes, I wouldn't waste my time by lying to you." Micah smiled in deep relief.

Malia entered her room and stepped off her companion square, leaving it close to the door. Her cube mates turned their backs to her. It was a group gesture showing they weren't happy about her fight with Jackson. She did not care, though. She gathered her belongings and waited by her desk for further instructions.

The children heard the speaker in their cubes turn on. "Attention, students," the announcer said. "In an orderly fashion, everyone must mount their companion squares. They will take you to your new living quarters." The announcement repeated continuously.

The kids passed each other through the halls, all chattering about the fight and their cube reassignments.

Malia saw Micah coming from the other direction and arrived at their new cube simultaneously. They entered their new cube, closed the door behind them, and gave each other a high-five. They jumped around the room, shouting with joy.

"Woohoo! Living together is so much better than living with people we don't know!" Micah said.

The speaker in the cubes turned on again. "Students, please unpack your belongings. Due to the events of this evening, everyone will be eating dinner in their cubes."

Malia was unable to articulate her feelings of relief. She said aloud into the air, "Papa! We're going to make you proud. Wait and see."

"Sis, I saw you getting a little too comfy with the new girl?" "First of all, her name is Tanisha, and she is the only one who

had my back—thank you very much. And remember, we don't have any friends."

"I'm not cool with her brother. He says whatever comes into his head." Micah was defensive. "I always have your back, but I don't think we should fight. You punched him right in the face."

The twins picked the first dinner listed on the menu and were happy that it was soup, salad, and a roll.

"Brother, I say that we give Tanisha and Mondarius a chance. We always complain that we don't have even one friend."

"Well, you can go be friends. I don't think I want to." "Micah, I thought you liked them this morning?"

He sidestepped the question and changed the subject. "Don't you think it was weird how y'all were spiraling out of control and couldn't level out?"

Micah explained that during the fight, he could see demons up in the trees. "They locked their arms together and pointed their hands out toward you like they were holding guns—a two-for-one hit. They're coming soon and will hurt us as they promised."

Malia's response was interrupted by a doorbell sound from the monitor in their cube.

A man appeared, and he cleared his throat, "Children. Stand by. Dean Duckworth will be here shortly."

Malia was nervous and looked at her brother.

The Dean sat in a chair behind a large console that looked like a spaceship's control center. "Malia, Micah, this is a warning—Malia, because of your impulsive behavior this evening, you could have been seriously injured or died. You let others control your behavior like puppets." The twins knew she was right.

"As a Jumper, it is crucial that you think before you act. You are not only endangering yourselves, but you are also risking the safety of the entire Academy when you allow your emotions to rule you." She was stern with her.

The twins sat in silence as the Dean continued her reprimand. "This is not a good way to begin your journey, and I will not tolerate this kind of behavior.

I expected more from Saul's grandchildren, so I will be watching you both carefully. Consider this your only warning. You're dismissed."

Malia's mouth dropped open when she heard the mention of Papa's name. She hoped he didn't know what had happened. She was there to make him proud, not to bring shame to the family.

The Dean's admonishment humbled them both. The twins quietly unpacked their belongings, changed into pajamas, and slipped into bed.

It was late, and they were tired from all the events of their first day. They didn't say a word to each other. They were lost in their thoughts.

The twins in the forest past their curfew.
Illustration and Photography by Adrienne La Faye © 2022

CHAPTER
ELEVEN

FIRST DAY AT THE
ACADEMY

The morning came with a loud escalating alarm that startled Malia and Micah from their first night's sleep at the Academy. They dressed hurriedly in their required Academy uniforms. The colors were red, blue, and orange, but the coordinating neutral color was grey. The children could mix and match their outfits so each day's uniform could be different, and the children could express their style.

Malia was excited about the color selections. She put together a stunning combination, she knew, choosing an orange blazer, red shirt, gray skirt, red leggings, and blue shoes and admiring herself in the floor-to-ceiling mirror. She was incredibly pleased with the ensemble she put together.

Ms. Topperhead had told her to use the computer Clothes Selector to select the outfits she wanted to wear; however, she didn't know to choose the style of uniform as shown in the Selector. She thought she could mix and match her outfit. When she rode to her new class, she noticed that she was dressed differently from the other girls, but it still didn't faze her.

Ahead of her, Malia saw Jackson for the first time since their fight. She pretended not to notice him, but he hovered and waited on his square for her to pass him. He pointed at her and laughed, "You look like a rainbow! Who taught you how to dress?

Malia took in a deep breath and puffed up her chest. That's it. I'm seriously going to knock out this idiot. Her hot temper swelled inside her.

She passed a girl with a face that looked like she smelled rotten eggs. She snickered at her friend. "Gurl, come on, we don't want to be associated with her and that fake diva outfit."

Malia bit her tongue. She didn't have time for stupid.

Micah smiled at Malia, and she knew his grin. He's relieved that she refrained from starting another fight. They were under strict surveillance.

Malia looked for their room number and realized they were following the same wannabe Diva girls. They were all assigned to the same teacher. Malia tried to shrug off, dismounted her companion, and walked toward the classroom.

Malia stood in the doorway, and her mouth dropped open, astonished by what she saw in front of her. She was enchanted by the explosion of bright, vibrant colors in hues of blue and red and the shape of its space. It was an oblong, starshaped capsule with six points. This classroom itself was a dream. This couldn't be real. She felt like she had just walked inside a twinkly star way up high into the heavenly sky.

Its ceiling had one point that shot straight up into a starshaped window. From the window, the walls were covered with shimmering midnight blue, the color you see on a moonlit night.

The dark nighttime color gradually faded to lighter blue hues of indigo, an alluring azure blue ocean, then softened to a cerulean blue that you see on a bright, cloudless day on the equator horizon.

This effect had a soothing, calming feeling of peace and confidence; Malia could already feel her anger shift to tranquility.

The sides of the star capsule pointed straight out, one to the left and one to the right. Malia shifted her gaze toward the floor. It was a fiery vermillion, a bright scarlet red color that contrasted the midnight blue ceiling. Her eyes slowly traced up the sides of this star capsule.

The colors were vibrant and almost hurt her eyes. She could vividly see each hue of red, which faded to juicy orange, then finished to a bright yellow—the color of the hot sun that stings you on a midsummer's day. She squinted her eyes. Oooo...I might go blind if I stare too long!

The hues of cerulean blue and bright yellow joined and delicately blended to a soft grass green within the points of the stars on each side of the room, giving it the look of a green horizon between the blues and the reds.

OMG! These were all the colors of the earth and sky on a perfect day.

The room had the feeling of being big and small at the same time, probably because of the points of the star that shot out in six directions from the center of the room. If it were a plain ole' square room, I'd be claustrophobic.

In front of her, she saw that the room was longer than wide. Both sections of columns fanned out directly across from each other. On the floor in front of the class was a giant star that perfectly matched the room's colors.

The teacher's desk and chair were centered in the middle and faced the children.

She turned her attention to the designated seating. It was like being in a movie where each row was one step higher than the other. Two columns of desks with a wide aisle divided the boys from the girls. The riser of each step glowed with a soft light. Another safety precaution, she thought. Micah would fall over his big sloppy feet.

The children were slow to find their desks. They were all enchanted with this room and marveled at its shape and colors, which could only be in the magical world of Dream Jumpers.

Malia looked around for Tanisha and spotted her already in her seat. Malia gave her a wave, and Tanisha returned the greeting. Malia checked the seating chart in her orientation packet and saw that her desk was next to Tanisha.

Tanisha spoke first, "This room is dope." "It's lit."

"Yo, gurl how ya doing today?" asked Tanisha.

Malia felt embarrassed but could sense Tanisha's sincerity. "I'm good. I wish I could have made him choke on his words, but he's not going anywhere soon."

"I heard you started the fight with him. Is that the truth?" "Well, you could say that, but I had an excellent reason." "Shame the devil. Tell the truth," Nudged Tanisha.

Malia explained the mishap. "I don't want to keep talking about it, so can we let it go for now?"

Tanisha responded so gently, "I understand. I'm glad I had your back."

Malia nodded and thanked her again. She didn't understand why the girl was so sweet to her, but she was grateful for her kindness.

Malia looked around for her brother, who had a desk beside Mondarius. The two boys weren't speaking to one another.

She wondered if Micah made him angry last night by ignoring his questions. The teacher entered the room, and Malia watched as she slipped on a silky black robe, the kind that judges wear. Despite its long zipper, the teacher left it open.

She appeared to be a young Latina woman. Her name is Ms. Perez. Malia liked her trendy red eyeglasses, and she loved the way the teacher was dressed.

Malia leaned over to Tanisha and whispered, "Diva alert."

"Eh, it's so so." Tanisha shrugged. She didn't care too much for her style. Malia envied her stylish look. She was hip and up to date.

The teacher wore a floral blouse under a cute orange jean jacket and a pink skirt to her knees that complimented her striped tangerine and fuchsia leggings.

She wore shiny green boots that reflected the lights in the room. Mrs. Perez was working on her wardrobe, Malia thought. The teacher set her books on her desk and was ready to teach. The door swung open behind the teacher, and Jackson was huffing and puffing.

"I'm sorry for being late. I overslept, and it won't happen again."

"What's your name?" Ms. Perez turned and peered over her eyeglasses. "Don't make this a habit."

"Jackson," he said and quickly took a seat.

Mrs. Perez directed the children's attention to the books she placed on each desk before their arrival. The kids moaned as if she had just introduced them to the 32-volume of The Encyclopedia Britannica, but there were only five books, and they weren't too thick.

A packet was placed on top of the books that included the list of required classes for their first term. They had also been given an electronic reading tablet. It was clearly labeled, so there was no mistaking: ABSOLUTELY NO INTERNET ACCESS. Malia thought they would at least have Internet here.

Mrs. Perez asked the students to take out the class schedule from their packets.

CLASS SCHEDULE:

1. **Academy Philosophy & History 101**
2. **Dream Jumping Theory 101**
3. **World Languages 101**
4. **Science & Mathematics 101**
5. **Fine Arts & Music 101**
6. **Each student must memorize:**
7. *The Dream Jumper's Oath.*

Ms. Perez waited for silence while the children chattered, shuffled papers and looked at their first-term curriculum. She stood dead center in the room, directly in front of the aisle. Her posture was upright and straight, and her feet were firmly planted on the floor. Her hands clasped behind her back.

"Why is it important for you to receive a Dream Jumpers education?"

Hands went up, rapidly waving, each side trying to get the teacher's attention. She pointed to a little boy sitting at the front middle desk. "Before you answer, Mr. Riddle, stand up and speak up."

The young Riddle child was ecstatic that he was the first to be picked and gave the teacher the widest smile he could muster. He cupped both hands behind his back, just like the teacher. "Because we need to learn what the old school people knew, don't make the same mistakes and maybe show us some shortcuts." The boy smiled gave his answer, sat down, and folded his arms over his chest, very proud of himself.

Malia looked at the kid and rolled her eyes. He was over the top with himself. She could not believe his confidence. Was he always like that?

His response amused Ms. Perez. "Why is the Dream Jumpers Pledge important for everyone to memorize?"

Not one soul dared to attempt the answer. "The pledge is your commitment to life as a Dream Jumper forever, and it is your understanding that you cannot switch to another call. It would help if you respected your assignments with honor and truth and never intentionally harm any of your charges.

You're committing to be respectful and obey Dean Duckworth and follow all the institutional rules and guidelines of the Academy. Are there any questions?"

No one said a word.

"This is your chance to leave right now if you feel you cannot live up to our standards." She paused for a moment, waiting to see if anyone would leave. No one did.

"Listen carefully to my instructions before you begin this next exercise. Pick up your tablets and push the button marked PLEDGE. The Academy oath will appear on each of your screens." She waited for the children to complete this instruction and turn their attention back to her before proceeding.

"Stand up, raise your right hand, and read what is on your screens. At the blank line, say your name. Now, let us all take the pledge together on the count of three." Ms. Perez demanded their full cooperation.

THE ACADEMY DREAM JUMPERS PLEDGE

I _____, do pledge to respect, obey Dean Duckworth, and accept her as the only supreme ruler, and voice of the Academy.

I accept the call of being a Dream Jumper for life.

I pledge to defend the Dream Jumpers Academy of the World with my whole being from all harm and danger.

I will uphold the rules of the Academy and commit to always using my skills with dignity and integrity.

I will respect my twin, professors, classmates, and myself always. I will not damage or harm the school or any of its property.

I take the pledge without reservation, and I acknowledge that I will never disavow or separate or deny the Dream Jumper's lineage as my family heritage.

I _____, do swear my life to the Dream Jumper Academy of the World today and forever.

Malia peered over toward her twin, then back to Tanisha sitting next to her and glanced around at the rest of the kids. They were all proud to accept the sacred Dream Jumper Oath.

Malia was more than just pleased to be a Dream Jumper; she believed it was a remarkable job. One day she knew she would be the best Jumper at the Academy.

Voices buzzed through the class as the children chatted among themselves.

Tanisha exclaimed, "Hey, how cool was that?" "Yeah, not bad at all," Malia shook her head.

Ms. Perez signaled for them to sit, as she continued the first day's lesson.

"It's important for us to know that we are not alone. We have a culture like no other. We are the only ones who have been born into a society that solely helps to nurture and instruct children on how to follow their calling or if you like their dreams. How important is our job?" she asked the children.

Malia raised her hand. "Yes, Malia?"

Malia stood to answer this question, and she was eager to show off her fashionable outfit. The children did indeed notice her and began to whisper about her choice of colors. She started to speak in a small voice.

"Speak up, rainbow!" taunted a kid somewhere in the room. The entire class laughed out loud.

Ms. Perez shushed the class. "Quiet, now."

"We all need someone to support and believe in us." Malia sat and scanned the other side of the room to see which idiot called her a rainbow. Her eyes landed on Jackson. Yes, of course, it was

Jackson. She glared at him as he mouthed the word, "RAIN-BOW." Her eyes stayed glued to him until her stare turned him away.

"Malia, seriously, don't let him make you mad," whispered Tanisha.

"I'm not. By the way, do you want to eat lunch together?" "Yeah."

They talked to each other by passing notes back and forth, and for the first time in Malia's life, she felt like she had a friend.

"Now, this next question may be hard for some of you," Mrs. Perez continued. "Can anyone tell me about your special power?" An Asian boy stood up without raising his hand. "I can."

"Ok, go ahead, Mr. Chan. Everybody, please remember to wait until you've been called on."

"My gift is having an astute sense of reading minds." The boy continued. "Also, the word sense is another name for the gift." Malia looks over at him. She liked this kid's gift, only because she wished she could read minds too.

"When did you know you could read people's minds?"

"It started a couple of months ago. At first, I didn't believe it, and then I thought it is so awesome because I can see and manipulate people's thoughts. My mom saw a change in me and asked me how I could know certain things, so I said to her, 'I don't know how. I just can.'"

Hands popped up. Each student stood and told the class about their extraordinary gift, or sense as little boy Chan so astutely explained. There were children who had the gift of seeing the future, a gift of strength, the gift of healing, the gift of smell that alerted the Jumper when danger was near, the gift of healing, the gift of invisibility, the gift of mind-reading, gift of time-shifting, and gift to inflicting pain. The children in this class were unique, and Mrs. Perez knew that these were but a few of the extraordinary gifts chosen for Dream Jumpers all over the world. There was so much more.

Malia glanced toward her brother. Neither of them said a word about their gifts. Malia held tight to her gift. She remembered the warning she received from Dean Duckworth because she had misused her strength and agility. She didn't want some kid to think that she was bragging.

Micah's gift of seeing visions had incredibly improved in the brief time they had been at the Academy. He didn't want to say a thing, mostly because of the way the kids treated him since the cafeteria incident. Their classmates avoided him and his sister, except for Mondarius and Tanisha.

Malia leaned in towards Tanisha, and in a hushed tone, she asked, "Hey, do you want to know what my gift is?"

Tanisha nodded, then quietly ripped another piece of paper from her notebook. Of course, I do. Tell me.

Malia passed a note back to the girl. Well, I'm crazy strong. I'm super, duper strong, and I'm excellent at sports.

The girls continued the conversation through secret notes.

"I already knew that!" Tanisha responded. "I thought you were going to say something really wild."

"What's yours?" asked Malia.

Tanisha smoothed her blouse down and straightened her blazer. "I can make myself invisible."

Malia read the note and looked at Tanisha with surprise, waiting for her to whisper sike, I'm just kidding.

Tanisha made a nod toward her feet. Malia looked down under her desk, and Tanisha's feet disappeared up to her ankles.

Malia's jaw dropped. She wrote feverishly. "Now that's the best gift! How do you do that?"

Tanisha read the note, looked at Malia, shrugged, and shook her head. Quietly, she said, "I don't how. I just can."

Malia handed a final note back to the girl. "I get it. I'm the same way. It just happens. Can you do that to your body too?" The girl nodded yes.

CHAPTER
TWELVE

MR. POINSETTER'S
CLASS

Tanisha and Malia had one more class before lunchtime, so they waited on their companion squares for their brothers.

Micah wanted to avoid all confrontations, so both sets of twins hovered off in the corner to allow the other kids to pass. When the hall was empty, they slowly rode through the corridors. They were the last ones to make it to the next room.

The classroom was the same as the first. It too was a colorful starshaped capsule-like room with vibrant hues of blue and red. Mr. Poinsetter was a large African American man who had squeezed his massive body in a too tight seersucker suit. He wore a shiny gold pocket watch in his vest pocket. His hair was disheveled and the color of coal.

His eyeglasses sat on his forehead, and his nose flared when he observed the class. He held his posture with a boldness that said, I have the knowledge, and you'll have to work hard to acquire a sliver of the information that I possess. Malia was intrigued by the man.

Mr. Poinsetter squeezed his eyes shut and laced his drumming fingers on top of his big belly protruding beneath his vest.

"Imagine yourself in a place where the rules you were taught no longer exist. Things are less restrictive, your life takes on new meaning, and you can navigate effortlessly throughout the world."

His voice was as big as his body—a deep baritone that resonated within the room. He paused for a moment to clear his throat.

"Except for the usual rules of Good vs. Evil, you can do whatever your mind desires, and it can be used to cause someone harm. There are positive consequences as there are negative ones."

Malia's mind searched the possibilities at the same time it drifted into exotic imaginations.

"Now, keeping in mind that we all have free will that is always present, you chart your life course in any way you desire. BUT, in the world of Dream Jumping, you are deciding not only for yourselves but also for those you will be assigned to guide."

"Yep, that pretty much sums it up," confirmed the teacher.

Moaning and groaning filled the room because that kind of responsibility was daunting. Then the voice of a white girl startled them back to the present.

"Mr. Poinsetter, what happens to us when we do make a bad call? You know, like a mistake?"

The teacher squeezed his left eye shut while his right eye fluttered like a fan blowing air, a slight smile eased up in the edges where the lips meet the cheeks. Malia was curious to hear his response.

"Can anyone respond to the question? Think, come on now think, what will happen to you if you make the wrong decision?"

Mr. Poinsetter picked Micah. His sister's eyes pinned on him, surprised that was chosen to answer. Micah stood and looked around the room. He wet his dry, chapped lips, and he began to speak.

His voice turned out a high-pitched squeal then sank back down to normal. His voice was going through puberty, and so he awkwardly shook his head, cleared his throat, and proceeded to answer.

"I guess we would have to fix the error. It would also make me more careful before I'd tell the kid to do anything. I would research, asks lots of questions, and then decide. When I mess up, I'd try and make it right as fast as I could."

He wiped the sweat from his upper lip with a new handkerchief he chose from the Clothing Selector in his cube. He sat back down in his chair. Mr. Poinsetter looked around the room. The silence was deafening.

"Did everyone hear that? Yes, that is precisely what you must do. You will have to work doubly hard to set things right. There are no exceptions to the Jumpers' law. Do it right or get it right. No one wants to hinder a child from reaching individual goals.

Everyone, please do not forget this. The skills that you acquire will equip you to handle different situations, along with your natural gifts."

"I have a question, Mr. Poinsetter," little Mr. Riddle says. "Yes, Mr. Riddle?"

"Why are kids helping kids? Doesn't it make more sense for adults to help them?"

"Yeah," snipped someone on a higher level of the star. "That does make better sense."

The children began to speak in soft whispers agreeing with this Riddle kid.

"What a great question, Mr. Riddle, I am so happy you asked that. Can anyone answer the question?"

Micah observed the teacher. Mr. Poinsetter's hands thumped on his ample stomach as he bent forward to gaze at his feet, waiting patiently for someone to answer.

Brianna put her hand up. "I think I know why."

Mr. Poinsetter looked up and over to the girl. "Yes, you there, take a stab at it."

She stood. "The reason why it's important for kids to help kids . . . Well, seriously who else is better to handle another one of us? Besides, we go through things our parents never had to go through, and they sometimes don't have a clue how to help us."

The class broke out in an uproar of applause. Malia felt comforted by what she said. We're going through things that our parents never had to deal with. She ignored the fact that it came from her enemy. The class was pumped up. Mr. Poinsetter acknowledged her by saying, "Another great answer. Ok, everyone, settle down."

"Next," shouted Mr. Poinsetter. "Who can tell me what you know about the Wrathtors?"

A flurry of hands thrust up, and everyone knew about them. Poinsetter chose Mondarius to answer. "They're evil entities trying to do away with the Academy and us."

"You have a grasp of the subject. Continue on Mr. Dewberry."

That's all Mondarius needed to hear. "Well, it began back in the year 1805. It was the first time that Wrathtors attacked the academy. It was horrible and devastating to all the new Jumpers. The Academy suffered badly, but because of the Dean's strategic planning, they pulled through the attack. Jumpers are always ready.

The Dean ordered small ships to be built and equipped with supplies that would last for months until they could return to rebuild the school."

Malia and the class and Mr. Poinsetter listened and were mesmerized by Mondarius's ability to tell a great story about the most boring information.

"Sooo, there are these evil things are out there…" Mondarius slowly turned to face the class, and he pointed his finger at every other child. "To kill you, and you, and you. That's right. I said it, when given the opportunity, they even kill children."

Some children held their breath, others squinted not to see his jesters, others have cupped hands over ears, and of course, there were a lot of oohs and ahhs. Malia slyly looked at Jackson, and even though he was not trying to interrupt the speaker, he was afraid too. Mondarius was just that good at storytelling.

The boy jumped up on his desk and bellowed out. "Don't fear little ones; they didn't win the war. That's right we won, so when you hear the alarm system screeching at you at Dark-thirty or high noon, remember to run to your cubes and suit up."

He bowed with his left arm bent across his waist and jumped off his desk and sat down and laughed with pure unadulterated joy when the class stood and clapped for him. "Y'all are making me blush, stop it. Go on and sit down. I appreciate your love." He was a born actor, and it was evident to everyone who'd ever listened to him speak.

After all that exhilarating information, Mr. Poinsetter dismissed the class for the day. The children ran out of the classroom and cautiously stepped on their companion squares.

Malia remembered she was eating lunch with Tanisha and sighed with relief. She had a friend.

CHAPTER
THIRTEEN

TEAM JUMPING

Micah looked at his class schedule. Today's class was Theory in Practice 101. Micah read everything he could get his hands on, so he at least could understand the concept of transference. He was determined to be ahead of today's lessons. It was the class all Dream Jumpers waited for—flying around campus. Well, except him. Flying was the first skill they would all need to master to possess the functionality to transfer from their world to the dream world.

According to the flying manual on his tablet, Micah learned that to be considered a good Jumper, all children needed to discern, teach, persuade, encourage, and become quick studies for all professions and environments. He stopped when he read that there was a difference between Jumping and flying.

Micah read to the very end. He didn't want to miss a word. The book explained that children should not worry about acquiring these traits all at once. Over time, as they matured, so would their skills and each attribute advanced at the speed of the Jumper.

Micah felt a little relief knowing he would eventually master flying and jumping.

Practice makes perfect was one of the school's mottos.

Micah was confident he understood the entire process, but the physicality would be his challenge. He had written his shortcut notes on his notepad and felt right about his study time.

The whole class was now in the athletic pod, waiting anxiously to begin flying and more Jumping lessons. There were sixty students in the class and three instructors. The course was divided into six groups of ten children. The children were split evenly between three instructors, and each had twenty students plus an upperclassman student leader.

A student leader walked to Malia, Tanisha, and Micah, Mondarius and another boy and girl grouped together. He was a pimple faced white lanky student, about eighteen years old, with stringy brown hair and translucent skin. Micah stepped as close as he could to watch everything he said and did.

First, the student leader instructed them on how to fly at the correct speed to jump. "You must reach the impact speed of 325 BEYGO, or you're gonna miss the portal."

The leader mounted his square with grace and reverence. It meshed with his body. He was the square, and the square was him. They were one. None of them had witnessed this before. They all had just stood on the companion squares.

Micah watched as the older kid's body jutted forward and tilted about a foot in front of him. His feet seemed to be glued to the square. He shot up in the air with so much thrust that, for a few seconds, they didn't see him. He reached the top of the stained glass atrium and was back down so fast that most of the students were still looking up for him.

He cleared his throat to get their attention, which startled Micah, and he flinched because he was always looking up at the ceiling. He looked over at his sister. She wasn't fooled. Her eyes were shining with new possibilities.

"Everybody listen to me, this is important. You will all have multiple opportunities to practice, so no pushing or shoving, your turn will come. Raise your hands if you believe you are already a good flyer and want to show off your stuff."

Not a peep or stirring from any of them. Of course, Micah knew his answer but couldn't get his nerve up. He was not ready to fly, not this SOON and NOT IN FRONT OF THE WHOLE CLASS.

A couple of the kids raised their hands to be the first to fly, but he called Malia to come to the front. "You, let's see what you can do."

Malia responded with confidence, "It's cool. I don't mind being the first one."

Micah crossed his arms tightly over his chest. If his sister did well, he was fine.

Malia winked at him as she stood on her square. Taylor, the student leader, stood next to her, adjusting the right slant for her body and the placing of her feet.

"Remember this before you fly," he instructed. "The square and you are one, and it will take you as far as your mind will allow."

Malia concentrated hard and psyched herself up to do her best. In one swift move, she twisted her head right to the left, cracking her neck bones, then lifted and rotated her shoulders. Her chin was down to loosen her upper body muscles.

Confidently on the square, her torso leaned forward, and she flashed up like a rocket. She shot up so fast that no one saw her rise and fly. Taylor searched up and around for her. He placed his hands on his waist, but his top lip, and quietly waited.

"Hey, guys! I'm behind you, did you not see me come down?"

Taylor turned around fast and then forward, seeing Malia standing behind him. The magnitude of her speed was unbelievable.

Micah cried out in disbelief. "NO WAY, you left and came back that fast! I didn't see a streak or anything! When the leader flew, at least I saw him for a couple of seconds." The small group hooped and hollered with amazement.

Malia graciously smiled. The leader gave her a high-five. Taylor announced, "Pay attention everyone. That was exceptional flying, and you will all be able to do so too. So, don't worry, it comes with time."

Tanisha said to her, "Gurl, show me how you did that because I need to be that fast too. You know I'm your wing girl." She flashed her a wide, bright smile.

"Can you please lower your voice? I'm not supposed to teach anybody."

Taylor overheard the girls talking. "Go ahead and show her how to fly. You're good enough to lead too. As a matter of fact, go ahead and teach three of the students and make sure your brother is one of them."

She chose her twin, Tanisha, and Mondarius.

The Jumpers in the Athletic Conditioning Pub observed cocky Jackson and his antics. He was the next to fly.

The stillness and quiet were so thick that only a sharp sword could sever the sound bubble. His square lifted a few inches, then sat down. "Whoa, what just happened?" said one of the kids. The others exhaled and waited.

"I have a question. How high can I fly? I mean, is there a limit?" Jackson asked.

Taylor shook his head, "You can go as far as your mind will take you."

Malia wanted to shout out, there's no way you can reach my altitude, but she made a promise that there wouldn't be any more fighting from her. So, instead, she let out an intentional crazy loud yawn that broke the trance in the Pub. She thought to herself, ooh, the idiot is flossing. Hurry up and finish!

Jackson held thumbs-up, leaned forward, and flew fast up and fast down, but everyone in the class could see him during his entire flight. It was a good flight without a hiccup, but he didn't get a high-five, and the leader didn't suggest that he help anyone.

Malia had her hands on her hips and watched the idiot's first attempt at flying. She gave Jackson a smirk and then a big smile that was almost a laugh. He was irate. He resented the lack of reaction he received, and he did not like being beaten out by a girl, especially Malia.

Jackson yelled out, "Hey, you leader, can I teach someone how to fly?"

Taylor poked his head up while giving a lesson to another child. He paused, "No, no not this time but maybe the next session. You did great though."

Malia quietly watched as the bully began a tantrum. The leader's response made Jackson angry. He thrust his hands into his jacket pockets and kicked his left foot at something that Malia could not see.

He turned and started badmouthing the leader and Malia to his foolish friends.

Malia turned back to her trainees and ignored Jackson as they continued training. Malia kept a watchful eye on the angry boy and her twin. Her brother was baffled and upset by Jackson's increasing anger.

They had to be painstaking alert, as not to get into any trouble they were still being monitored by Dean Duckworth.

Tanisha whispered to their small group, "I can't believe he asked to teach somebody when he wasn't even that good."

"You ain't lying about that," said Malia.

"Let's get back to work," said Malia. "Guys, the first step —believe in yourself and trust your companion like you do your twin. That's how I did it."

It was Tanisha's turn, and she did an excellent job. She learned how to become one with her companion. Mondarius did as well, too.

Now it was Micah's turn. His sister placed her hands on his shoulders and looked directly into his eyes. "Micah, will you do what I tell you to do, and you'll be fine? Whatever you do, don't try, and take control. Let it happen naturally."

She sounded confident. "You told me how this works after you read the entire manual. You got this, okay brother?"

He stepped on his companion square, leaned forward, and thought of nothing else but synchronizing with his square then, he shot straight up. Micah looked up but made the mistake of looking down and became afraid he was going to fall. Whoosh!

He returned too quickly and made it only halfway up to the target goal, but it was the highest he had ever flown.

Malia gave him a high-five. "Dude, you did great, and you didn't fall. Next time you will go higher."

Micah was about ready to say thanks when he heard Jackson. "That kid will never get it."

Moon, Brianna, and Star all had a good laugh at Micah and gave him a long stare. It was intimidation at its finest.

"I'm good," says Micah, "so, let's forget them." He knew his sister had tried to build up his confidence, and he wasn't going to disappoint her by giving up.

Mr. Dozen was the instructor of another class, and he was talking about what to do and what not to do. "If you cannot perfect Jumping, bad things could ensue."

He explained all the things that could go wrong in Dream Jumping. "Missing the jump entirely means not entering the dream at all. It's about velocity and accuracy."

Mr. Dozen enunciated his words slowly and clearly to ensure the children understand. "Entering a dream at the wrong time, when the child is still awake, can emotionally scar a child for life. That would be the worst-case scenario.

And, of course, jumping into the wrong person's dream." His voice was emphatic. The children understood.

In a hushed voice, Malia said to her brother, "I'll be glad when this class is over."

"Me too," Micah agreed. Tanisha rolled her eyes and blew out the air she had been holding. Micah started to think the girl might be a good friend to his twin. He glanced at Mondarius and thought to himself, I should find out if this dude is smart or not.

"If any of those things happen," said Mr. Dozen, "it will throw off the whole assignment. Who would take a Jumper seriously? Who would believe in a clumsy, inexperienced Dream Jumper? First impressions are the only impressions." His thick pointer finger poked toward each child.

The children were given more work assignments before being dismissed. Micah peeked at his tablet for the next lesson.

12 DREAM JUMPING RULES

1. The Jumper's only mission is to aid the child. A jumper can not take the child's job and do it for them at no time.
2. Before jumping into their dream, the Jumper cannot go anywhere the subject hasn't experienced (people, places, and things).
3. A jumper can venture without the child anywhere the subject has dreamt. That includes their living space, school, and all surroundings.
4. The Jumper must be in the subject dreams of going to places where the child has never ventured.
5. The Jumper can have conversations with the subject, even when they're awake.
6. The Jumper can take the subject anywhere to teach or expose the child to the lucid dream state needed information.
7. The Jumper must have physical contact with the subject's hand or body to fly them around in the dream.
8. The Jumper can watch the subject perform and dream without knowing they are under observation or surveillance by the Jumper.
9. The Jumper can perform any task necessary to help develop the child while the child is in a lucid dream state.
10. The Jumper cannot enter a subject's body unless they are in a transparent dream state.
11. Jumper's subject IS NOT ALLOWED to operate a square companion at any time. There are no exceptions to this rule. (It has never happened)
12. JUMPERS AT NO TIME ARE ALLOWED TO INJURE ANY CHILD. Fighting is allowed only for the safety and well-being of the child subject.

Later that evening after dinner, Micah and Malia squared it back to the Athletic Pod so Micah could practice his flying. Malia took off as soon as she entered the gym. Micah called out to her. "How are you doing that? Show me again!"

Malia came down and took Micah by the elbow and told him not to be afraid; she was there and would not let him fall. "Micah you've got to stop being logical. Brother, you must stop thinking about bad things. Concentrate only on flying, and before you know it, you'll be doing it."

Micah wanted to trust his sister, so he tried what she told him. He started out slow and was determined to get this right. Micah cleared his mind and thought only about flying. He leaned forward and let go, he was operating well.

He was much smoother than during class. The twins were flying side-by-side for a while when other kids came in to practice as well. Every one of them improved, and Micah could feel his selfconfidence growing.

CHAPTER
FOURTEEN

WRATHTORS: DEFENSE AND SPACE PODS

In the middle of the night, the Academy's alarm in the corridor sounded off and penetrated the children's cubes. It was excruciatingly louder than the morning alarm. The sound whirled continuously like the loudest five-star alarm fire trucks.

The twins bolted straight up and covered their ears with both hands. The sound pierced their ears. Around multi-colored light fixed high up on the wall spun its colors around the room. The sun was blindingly bright. Malia shielded her eyes from the sudden light and looked at the clock. It was 3:27 a.m.

"Micah, what's happened?" Malia screamed to be heard over the deafening whirl of the alarm. Micah shook his head with uncertainty.

He shouted out to the smart computer in their cube. "Computer! What's going on"?

A woman's voice responded. It was pleasant but firm. "This is a full battle alert. Mount your companion square at once. The CAMA will fit you in your MBS. You will be taken to your

designated bunker pod. This is not a drill. Your suits will be lowered to dress you. Stay on your squares."

"Micah! What do you think is going on?" Malia and Micah jumped out of their beds and sprinted to their squares, and waited as they were told.

The twins looked at each other in sheer terror. "Computer-aided mechanical arm!" he shouted. "I read about it in the manual! They are going to help us put on our military battle suits! They turn us invisible during battle!"

The ceiling slid open. The twins looked up and watched as two mechanical arms lowered down from a cerulean blue haze. The CAMA was made of mirror finished titanium that was fully jointed at the elbow, wrist, and hand with fingers. Suspended from the fingers of the CAMA was a suit that each Jumper must wear during emergency combat. Both of Malia's hands were balled up into fists.

As the suits lowered down, the voice soothingly continued the instructions. Malia could not believe how calm the voice sounded, given the emergency they faced.

"These suits are for your protection," explained the voice. "They are military chameleon suits. They change color to match the environment around you. This is to conceal and protect you from the evil enemy."

Malia watched the mechanical arms descend from inside the ceiling as the pleasant voice continued the instructions. The CAMA was to dress and fit a suit on each child.

The twins lifted their arms straight up. A mottled brown space age suit slipped down over the head and arms of each child simultaneously. The arms pulled the suits over their torsos and legs. They looked like shiny silver dresses with attached boots, but there were two splits down the middle, on the front and on the back, that connected to form the legs.

They remained in position while the fingers of the CAMA pulled down on the suit bodice. The children were instructed to put their feet into the suit boots, and the CAMA clamped the legs clasps.

The suits were made of a thin aluminum fabric light enough to fly but strong enough to protect them in battle. Each arm simultaneously withdrew into the blue haze and returned with a head cap clutched between its mechanical fingers.

The hat looked like a mixing bowl, perfectly round on the top with tiny holes on each side to allow the child to hear.

The hand lowered to place the cap on each child's head. Malia felt like she was inside an oven. Oh, brother. How am I going to survive in this suit?

During this chaos, the alarm continued to siren out its warning, and the light spun colors around the room. The voice explained the importance of the head caps and to never take them off. It would keep their heads invisible. But the children could not think straight. They were panicked.

Malia shouted to her brother. "Whatever is going on, this is serious."

Before Micah could answer, the door to their cube automatically opened. The twins quickly jetted down the corridor. The jolt of the companion squares temporarily startled the children off balance, but they quickly regained their stance.

They were powerless over their squares. They whisked through a series of corridors. When they reached the highly guarded passage, the NO-GO ZONE, their squares began to reduce their speed.

The corridor was lined with ten red and white doors, five on the right and five on the left. Each entry reads RESTRICTED. They had been warned about these doors. It was clearly stated in the orientation manual never to open any of them.

The twins stopped suddenly at the last door on the right—pod Ten. There was a double-lock, the door slid up, and the children were shuttled inside.

Malia was relieved to see her two new friends, and she and Micah moved over to Tanisha and Mondarius in the same emergency pod.

All the children in the pod were stunned as well. They nervously chatted about the screaming alarm and bright lights, the weird arm thing that came out of the ceiling, and their crazy silver suits. It was pandemonium inside the pod. Malia looked over at her brother and saw that he was finally participating in conversation, especially with Mondarius.

The Jumpers throughout the Academy were all assembled in their assigned pods. The Jumpers in Pod Ten waited anxiously for the squad leader to give them their following instructions. As they mingled together, each child slowly became invisible, hands and arms, then their bodies, legs, and feet all vanished. The children were in wonderment as they watched each other disappear before their eyes. They could feel their bodies, but they could not see them.

The chatter in the room grew louder. Oooo . . . Oh my goodness . . . Whoa, check this out. Hey man, where'd my arm go?

Dude, you got no feet. Ha-ha ha ha!

"Listen up, children!" Their squad leader yelled to quiet them down but to little effect. "This is not the time to play! We are going to be attacked! Shush. Be quiet, Y'all! Listen to me. Your suits are preparing you for defense!"

Malia was hot and claustrophobic under this crazy chameleon military astronaut looking mixing bowl suit. She could feel one trickle of sweat run down her forehead, and the back of her neck became wet. Without much thought to the importance of the cap,

DREAM JUMPERS THE INHERITANCE | 121

she removed it from her head and shoved it under her arm, like a football.

The girl understood the suits were equipped with technology that enabled the Jumper to see the enemy without being discovered. She looked around her. Oh, man! This was entirely on fleek. The pod seemed empty, but she could distinctly hear each of the children talking.

Tanisha spoke to her, although she could not see her. "Yo, hurry up and put that whatchamacallit thing back on so your big ole' satellite head will disappear." She teased and giggled. "All we see is your head bobbin' around with nothing attached to it."

"Tanisha, how do you know about this stuff?" Malia grumbled while she topped her head with the mixing bowl.

"Dang, you already forgot about my gift? Gurl, if you remember anything about me, you should remember that I know everything about invisibility."

She paused and waited for Malia to answer and, with slight indignity, said, "You remember now?"

"My bad. I forgot in all this chaos! Promise, I won't forget again."

Malia was happy that Tanisha had become her new best friend forever. They didn't argue and, in the little time they had known each other, they almost felt like sisters. Tanisha came to her side when no one else would.

Malia had never had another kid treat her kindly and so sweet and friendly. She swore to herself that she would have Tanisha's back whenever she needed her.

Tanisha and her brother, Mondarius, were from New York City. They were fearless. They grew up in an area where confrontation was standard. They had to either fight or flight. At this moment in Pod Ten, the two sets of twins realize they are family and will hang together all the time.

The ear-piercing alarm stopped. The children were visible again. They looked down at their bodies and then toward each other in amazement. No one had ever had this magical experience, except for Tanisha, of course.

Quickly two squad leaders entered Pod Ten and told the children to remain on their squares. They were being transported to the Defense Chambers, where they would be assigned a Battle Pod and then be given their emergency duty responsibilities.

"Hey! Y'all didn't think we were really in a war zone?" Mondarius was the only one who spoke up. "I figured this wasn't the end game because there ain't any weapons or food supplies." He pauses and looks at the group, puzzled. "What?"

The children looked with disbelief.

"I play a lot of war video games," explained Micah. "Dude, there is a lot more we need than weapons and food supplies."

Malia was stunned and glad that her brother spoke up, letting the kids see whom she saw daily. She could tell the others were interested in the information he was sharing.

Malia and Micah were in the corridor gliding side-by-side on their squares to the Defense Chamber when she asked him, "What's up with you? You, okay?"

He winced and shook his body beneath the suit like he got the chills. "They're not telling us the truth about what we're up against."

"Did you have a vision?"

"I dreamt about this last night. It was not nice." He nodded. "This is exactly what I've been trying to tell you about . . . those things."

Malia began to put two and two together: Micah's visions of monsters and the upcoming battle. She flew her square fast enough to catch up with the squad leader, Taj.

"Excuse me, are we fighting the Wrathtors?"

He gave her a look of surprise. "Kid, did you forget what you were taught about the alarms and the Wrathtors?"

She shook her head and mouthed the word No. Her lips extended outward in no slight pout that started from the corners of her mouth.

Taj stopped his square in the middle of the corridor and told his Jumpers to gather around him.

"Listen up! For all of you who may have forgotten . . ." He looked to Malia as he said this. "I'm going to tell you the truth, and I'm not going to hide a thing from you."

"We are wearing battle gear! We are in battle mode! The Wrathtors have entered into our planetary orbit, and our Academy will be attacked."

"Follow my commands and move quickly. Keep your eyes peeled. If you see them, smell them, or hear them, take it as a warning. They are close to you.

They may grab you and do you harm. If the Wrathtors do, fight! The panic button on the wrist of your suit will alert us that you are in trouble."

"And do not forget to USE YOUR GIFTS as defense weapons." He enunciated very slowly, so there was no mistaking what he was saying."

During the Taj's speech, Malia's mind wandered off, and she noticed her brother's eyes freeze onto something in front of him. She looked around him, but nothing. What was he seeing?

Malia quickly darted back in line with her brother. "Hey, I just saw that funny expression on your face. Tell me what you just saw; I want to help too?"

"Give me some time. As soon as I understand what it means, I will share it with the leaders."

"Dude, okay, but what if you get it wrong? This is some serious stuff now."

He shrugged his shoulders. "Let me do me."

Malia was ready for whatever came her way. She was fast and robust.

The Pod Ten group is led down another long corridor, further into the restricted areas, into a large round hall.

The children from the other emergency pods are already there and being herded by groups into large rectangular lifts that descend hundreds of feet beneath the school into the safety of the bunker known as The Defense Chamber.

Once below the surface of the Academy within the Defense Chamber, all Jumpers and staff were sectioned off and guided into separate Battle Pod Spaceships. The squad leaders referred to them as Battle Pods.

Malia tried counting the battle pods, but she could not get an exact count. There were too many.

A senior captain and first mate commanded the Battle Pod. On-board each pod was a doctor and a nurse, twenty longtime Jumper warriors, and twenty new Jumpers-in-training.

The Pods were equipped with essential supplies to sustain each person if the Academy was ever destroyed.

Once Malia was inside the Battle Pod, she whispered to Micah. "Dude, this is the place where they'll see your worth."

"Sis, I know. I got this. Trust me. I won't let' cha down, I promise."

"Shoot, I'm not worried about you," and she gave him a little nudge. "Hey, what did Papa always say?

WE HAVE EVERYTHING WE NEED INSIDE US." The twins whispered together their Papa's soul code just as he taught them.

They repeated it with sincerity, integrity, and with their heart.

Taj was also their Battle Pod Squad Leader, whose duty was to update their modus operandi, basically what would happen while they were in the pod. Malia wondered about his special gift. Maybe he could be a strong leader?

"Can I please have your attention?" Taj was at the pod's helm along with the captain. There was a massive control panel behind him with levers, compasses, and buttons of every color that were lit and in startup mode. Taj attempted to halt the group from their chatter. He waited until every eye was on him.

"This underground bunker is The Defense Chamber. We have 550 Battle Pod Spaceships. Each pod holds twenty-two students and twenty faculties. We have four hundred and six adult Jumpers who will be divided among the Battle Pods with the children Jumpers."

The children began to murmur. It never occurred to them that there were grownup Jumpers.

"If we come under attack and lose our Academy and spatial galaxy, the control behind me will be activated, and we will fly into outer space," The junior leader explained.

"These ships operate on generators and contain enough provisions to sustain each child and adult for at least five years, maybe more. There are beds for each of us, clean uniforms, and new shoes."

The Jumpers were silent. Not an utterance of a sound was heard.

"Once each Battle Pod enters outer space, it will morph its outer color to resemble a round multi-colored marble that will appear as a random planet to the Wrathtors."

Taj continued his speech while handing out small tablets to each of the Jumpers. "Through these tablets, you can read more about the Battle Pods. The fun stuff is on the VPS channel.

There are videos about the Battle Pod, your classroom lectures on Jumping, how to master your unique skills, and interactive video games that simulate battles with the Wrathtors.

All the Battle Pod Spaceships are fortified with the tools needed to battle the enemy. We have on board a galaxy GPS, power beaptrons that regenerate with ammunition beams, etcetera."

Taj held up a tablet and showed the children how to access the reading material and the VPS Channel. "Take a few moments to read chapter one, Battle Pods General Info. When you finish, peruse through the tablets to become familiar with them. Then you will be assigned your new duties."

Malia could only wonder why this had never happened in the Academy's history. Why now when we are here?

CHAPTER
FIFTEEN

THEY'RE HERE!

Ms. Topperhead oversaw the master roster. Malia could see her on the main ship's screen calling out the names of everyone on board and which Battle Pod they were assigned.

"Five adults, a teacher, administrator, chaplain, cook, and a military captain...." Malia stopped listening and began to think about what else she could offer to her Battle Pod.

Papa trained her to be healthy, fast, quick on her feet like a boxer, and fierce. She was ready to fight. Papa told her it was one thing to train and another to fight. He prepared her since she was a petite girl, and she learned quickly, and after he died, she kept up with her daily practices to keep in shape and was ready.

Her thoughts of fighting reminded her that she needed to talk to her brother. She found him scribbling notes in his notepad in the Battle Pod and knelt beside him.

"Micah, I have to say something."

The children were waiting for their new instructions, so they had a moment to talk.

"We're cool with each other, right?" she asked. Micah nodded with his head down, reading his notes.

"What I'm saying is . . . don't leave me standing alone like you did that night at the fight." She said it as gently as possible not to rile him up.

Micah put his pen down in his notebook and looked at her. "Sis, didn't I apologize for that? I'm sorry. I didn't know how to handle it, and I kept seeing those things. I got it now. We'll cover each other's back. Deal?" The brother and sister fist pumped in solidarity

She doubted him, though. He didn't like to fight, but she would give him the benefit of the doubt.

That afternoon the new Jumpers gathered around Taj in the Battle Pod. He reaffirmed the need to keep close to their squares and trust their power.

Malia could see how the squares proved to be more than transportation and navigational devices. At Malia and Micah's junior-level they weren't allowed to control and fire off the beaptrons for battle. Only the officers on board were assigned that duty.

During Taj's lecture, an announcement came through the intercom. The Wrathtors had arrived!

"Stay alert! Stay alert! The Walls of Defense have been placed around our perimeter. The Wrathtors cannot penetrate them, but we still need to be on our game for combat."

"Where there is Good, Evil will follow," the quote was written throughout the facility. Overall, the crew among the 550 Battle Pods was a potent force that would forge a sustaining and debilitating blow to overcome the evil.

Malia watched her brother. He could see the demons flash around outside their Pod. His eyes were alert and intense. It was as though someone had turned on a light switch inside his head. His power to see had transformed him into a battle-ready mode. Micah was alive and controlled.

She watched him move quickly around the Pod, instructing the kids to always stick with their squares.

"No matter what comes, no matter what happens, DO NOT separate from your square. Just stay on it and low to the ground." Malia could not believe that her meek, introverted brother was in action. Her eyes were stuck on him like white on rice. She watched as he paused in mid-air and cocked his head to listen to something outside the Pod.

The Jumpers and leaders began to hear the threatening screams of evil from outside. They could feel their power as though the Pod was in a compression chamber pressing against them. Malia had a sickening feeling in her gut that rose into her throat, and she began to gag. She needed to remain composed, she thought. I've got to get it together. She stayed still and swallowed several times until the feeling of throwing up subsided.

An aura of bright golden and blue light surrounded Micah. His stance was now imposing. His gift to see was his tool to combat evil. He flew around the Pod as if his square was playing chess like maneuvers.

Malia's eyes were fixed on her brother and darted with each move he made. He gathered and relayed information instinctively from the evil outside, and he wasn't afraid. She didn't understand how he could do this, but she was in awe of his skill and his confidence. He was where he truly belonged.

Malia rushed to her defense position as she was instructed. She looked up at the monitors but could not see anything. Then she remembered that Micah's visions could be minutes or even days ahead of what was happening in real-time. Her thoughts were broken by a voice screaming from down below her.

It was Micah. "Brace yourselves! Get down! They're coming for us!" He scrambled from child to child telling them to lay down where they are. "There are hundreds of thousands of Wrathtors out there!"

Malia continued to stare at the monitors and waited to see something, anything. Then in a flash, the screen went dark. The captain angrily shouted to his crew. "Please tell me there's nothing wrong with our monitors! Tell me we didn't just lose power to our visuals!"

One of the female crewmembers spoke up. "Captain, we didn't lose power. I've checked the system, and everything is working correctly, as it should be."

Micah's voice was amplified and echoed throughout the ship. "Sir, it's the Wrathtors. They've entered our perimeter, that's why our screens went blank. They have swarmed over our galaxy and are trying to penetrate the Walls of Defense."

Within moments, the Pods deapontry were fired off. The young Jumpers hid under their bunks with their squares. The generators in the Pod were turned on.

BOOM!

The explosion came from within the Pod and reverberated outward. There was no monitor to observe, so Malia turned to watch her brother in action.

Micah could see everything outside Battle Pod and into the atmosphere. She heard him give the captain a play-by-play of the Wrathtors' movements.

"Here comes another one!" he shouted.

"Captain set deaptron S2 toward the south to southwest. They're coming at us from behind the cliffs."

There was rapid fire coming from the Pod. Bam Whooosh. Bang. BAM! BOOM! BOOM! BOOM!

"Captain, airstrike accomplished. The beaptrons intercepted the Wrathtors' long range missile and stopped it from fatally hitting the vessel."

Micah oversaw this battle. He was on top of his game, and he now understood how to use his unique skill of seeing. He was no longer afraid.

High pitched shrills faded into distant low moans as beaptrons fired beams that torched the Wrathtors. The moaning and hissing were an awful sound, and Malia once again was sick to her stomach and swallowed back her nausea.

The Walls of Defense proved to be a strong fortress for their world. It looked like a galaxy of many planets layered within circle after circle, like a lollipop until you get to the chewy center. But this wasn't sweet, Malia thought. The Walls of Defense were secure, right down to the inner circle.

Evil had retreated, but they may return another day to finish what they started.

The following day, the Academy worked on drills to continue training the newcomers to be their best defenders and to realize how their unique skills can be used to fight evil.

They were all tired, but they were pumped up, adrenaline continued to course through their bodies. They needed this extra energy to work throughout the week ahead.

They all grasped the fighting techniques well enough to satisfy the captain. When the vermillion moon arrived in two days, the Jumpers would continue with their scheduled classes in the Academy.

Chancellor Duckworth watched the Pods inside surveillance footage from the night before. The woman tapped her pointed fingernails on the console metal and watched how each child reacted to pressure, exhaustion, and danger. She was not disappointed with any of the children.

She was delighted, however, by one of the students she reprimanded only days before. Micah Crenshaw. He had no idea he was evaluated during the battle.

The Chancellor constantly surveyed each student until each child had mastered their skill and conquered their greatest fears. Her unique ability was to cultivate the advancement of every child who walked through the doors of Dream Jumpers Academy of the World.

CHAPTER
SIXTEEN

ACTRESS NATALIE

"Hey, you! Yeah, you. Stop running. I need to talk to you." Micah shouted at the little girl hoping she would stop. He wanted to stop flying after her. His square was moving at a moderate clip, but the child wouldn't stop running.

Malia spoke gently, "Little girl, why are you running?"

Malia was toe-to-toe with her and flying exceptionally well. The little girl kept running from them, but her tiny feet skipped, tripping her up.

She almost fell but steadied herself and kept moving. Malia sprung past the girl and descended in front of her. The little girl stopped. Her eyes were wide, questioning the reality of what she was seeing.

The twins had received their first assignment. Before they began, they acquainted themselves with the child's biography and created a game plan to help her achieve her dream. Malia read the girl's information aloud to her brother in their cube. Micah took careful notes.

> **Name:** Natalie Whitehead.
>
> **Age:** Nine years old.
>
> **Goal:** She wants to be an actress.
>
> **Obstacles:** She has no support; her mother works long hours; left alone.
>
> **Challenges:** She has never acted professionally; has no training; too young.
>
> **Strengths:** At five years old, she was play-acting. Memorizing lines comes naturally. She wants to be an actress ASAP. She is talented.
>
> **Summary:** She was unsupported, sad, needy, and clueless about how to proceed. However, she was determined to follow her call.

"I feel sorry for her already." Malia finished reading out her biography.

"We shouldn't feel bad for these chosen kids because their situation is about to change. Besides we don't want to be too easy for them. Right?" Not needing an answer.

"I was running because you were chasing me," replied little Natalie. "What did I do? Why are you chasing me?" She begins to slowly walk away, trying to ignore the presence of the twins.

The little girl was nine years old with brunette hair and bright green eyes. In her hand, she held a play booklet. She wore dirty blue jeans and a sparkly blue t-shirt with a jean jacket tied around her waist.

Malia took a closer look at the girl. She could see the fear in her eyes. Malia presumed that this was the first time she had witnessed someone flying.

So, Malia started again. "I didn't mean to scare you. I'm Malia, and I'm here to help. Aren't you Natalie?"

The girl looked bewildered. She wondered; how do they know my name? Instead, she said to them, "Yes, my name is Natalie, but I'm not supposed to talk to strangers even though you're a kid too."

Micah finally approached the two girls, landing his square next to Malia. He paused to huff and puff his breath in and out, nauseated, coughing, and spitting up loogies from the back of his throat.

Although he showed great ability to use his sense to see during the Wrathtor attack, he still could not balance his square, and the pace was too fast for him. Do not think about what could go wrong, just fly.

Malia's spoken words that reverberated in Micah's head. He knew he had improved, but he had to be perfect for graduates. One twin couldn't advance without his or her sibling. They were a team.

Once he regained his breath, his voice was loud and arguable.

"Little girl, why are you running away?"

Malia rolled her eyes. She half turned to him while keeping her eyes steady on the little girl. "Micah, stop screaming at her. Can't you see she's scared? She's never seen anyone fly before.

Micah responded, "Oh yeah, right, of course." He gave a weak apologetic smile. Malia tried to ignore his halfhearted agreement. Malia, on the other hand, was feeling fantastic. She had done a maneuver like an old schooler, and at the same time, it validated her calling.

While Malia continued to chat with the little girl, Micah stood in silence, not wanting to upset her further. "Let's go sit down and talk, ok? There is a park across the street." However, it was more like a strip of grass with a bench on a concrete sidewalk.

The twins on their squares escorted the little girl across the street.

"We're sorry." Malia looked at her brother hoping he would take the hint and apologize as well. "We didn't mean to scare you. We're here to help you."

Micah mumbled out "Ah, sorry," and was genuine in his apology, but he was still too antisocial to make it come across as sounding real. Natalie stared at the twins. She didn't say a word.

Malia continued, "We're Dream Jumpers. We've been sent to help you realize your dreams. We will make your dreams come true." Malia was joyful as she said these words for the first time. She gave Natalie a broad smile, bent down, and hugged the girl, like a big sister to a little sister.

Natalie's hug to Malia wasn't receptive to the friendliness. She was still questioning and disbelieving of these two flying teens. But her mama always told her to mind her manners and be polite.

"Thank you," she said.

Then little Natalie stood up and started to walk away.

"Where are you going?"

"I'm going home." Natalie's response was abrupt. "It's late. It was nice meeting you both, goodbye."

Malia had to think quickly, or they would miss their chance to talk to the girl. "You're dreaming, and right now your home in your bed."

Natalie stopped and turned to look at them, rapidly blinking her eyes.

Ooo... Kay. The lights are on, but no one is home. Malia wondered if the girl was emotionally abused in some way. Why wasn't she happy? They were there to take her sadness away.

"Natalie. You are dreaming right now. We are in your dream." Micah spoke up again, yet his voice was still raised. He enunciated each word deliberately and slowly as though she could not hear him. Yeah, that always works. Shout and talk slowly.

"Micah, she's not deaf. Stop yelling at her." Now it was Malia who raised her voice and deliberated her words to him. Apparently, he is not listening to me. But she unintentionally one ups him by talking out the side of her mouth so that the little girl won't hear her.

"If I'm dreaming, why are we outside if I'm supposed to be at home in my bed sleeping?"

Micah was in total agreement. "That does make sense. She has a point."

Okay, good. Whew. The girl knew how to reason and use logic. That was a good sign. She was smart. Malia believed they were now on a roll. But they weren't. The twins stood there frozen. Their minds were blank. Their first Dream Jumping lesson was forgotten:

How to convince a reluctant dreaming kid. The students all stared at each other, eyes blinking rapidly. Not knowing what else to do, Micah said goodbye to both.

Natalie turned and walked away until she dipped around the corner, and the twins slipped out of her dream.

CHAPTER
SEVENTEEN

"TMI" (Too Much Information)

"Bro, that went terribly wrong! It'll take us forever to be decent Jumpers," Malia complained.

"We just need a plan." Micah rubbed his face. "But where do we start?"

"I don't have a clue. Shoot, we need our own Dream Jumpers."

Malia cracked a joke that got Micah laughing along with her.

"But all jokes aside, we need help."

In their classroom, Mr. Jackknife waited for Malia and Micah to take their seats. He walked in a circle around the embossed granite star in the middle of the floor, careful not to step on it with his shoes.

He looked toward the class. "First, let's discuss what Micah did right and then what Malia did right. Secondly, after our positive feedback, we'll suggest what they can improve on."

Hands all across the room were raised up in the air. He pointed to a solidly built, very tall boy with bright red hair.

"Yes, you, please answer the first question."

"Malia is a superior flyer, and Micah's not a bad flyer either once he flew. When Malia showed empathy for the kid and told her she was sorry for scaring her, that was well done. Micah did a good job of supporting Malia, and they both knew when it was time for them to leave."

Because we made the kid wake up, Malia thought miserably.

"Good, good excellent observation," said Mr. Jackknife.

More hands rose to answer the question. Mr. Jackknife pointed to a little girl who was sitting across the aisle from her twin brother, who was as small as her. "Miss, yes you, go ahead," instructed the teacher.

The tiny white girl began to speak. Her voice was thick and husky, which surprised Malia. In fact, Malia thought her voice sounded like a boy's and was more commanding than the size of her tiny frame. She looked like the kind of kid most people would underestimate because she was small and wore a neatly pressed uniform. Her brown curly hair was gelled, pinned, and brushed to stay in place.

"Micah needs to believe in his flying ability. He's a lot better flyer than he thinks. Malia could have waited for Micah to catch up before approaching the girl. That's why they frightened her so badly. They flew after her and didn't present a united front." Her response made all the kids take notice of her. She was smart.

"Anything else, people?" asked Mr. Jackknife.

Micah stood up and said, "Mr. Jackknife?"

"Yes, Mr. Oliver?"

"I want to say that it was my fault. My sister did the jump right. Malia tried waiting for me, but I froze." He said, finishing his self-assessment. "I knew that it had to be precise timing to enter the

REM state while the dreamer is still in bed. The next dimension felt weird, and I blew it. That's why the girl left us and was dipping down the street, running like a chicken with its head cut off."

Scores of laughter broke out, including Mr. Jackknife, who raised his hand to hush the laughter.

"I'm pleased with you, Micah because you see how you can improve and admit you weren't ready." He paused his following statement. A matter of children still chuckles over Micah's joke.

"I want everyone's attention. If you don't get anything else out of my class . . ."

Mr. Jackknife stopped talking, walked to the chair behind his desk, and slowly sat down. The children noticed the frustration on his face. He waited for the class to simmer down.

"Well said," Mr. Jackknife explained. "Since the child is still asleep, you must wait and be ready for their dream to start again. But also remember not to disrupt the dream too much; it may cause a child to wake. Children, please get this," he continued. "Remember, everyone has a partner. No one is doing this alone because it's a joint twin effort.

The first meeting is the most crucial of all because we need to gain the dreamer's trust. Who's going to trust a late or ill-prepared Dream Jumper?"

He had the children's attention now, so he stood up and regained his position in front of the class.

"I'll tell you who. NO ONE. That's right. NO ONE. There's no 'I' in a team. Remember, you're also representing DJAW. You could get lucky. Some poor kid won't care. I can tell you right now that ninety-nine-point-nine percent of all kids are already dealing with personal problems and fears daily. The average kid isn't going to wait around for the two of you to get in sync. Pay attention to your sibling and always maneuver as a unit." Mr. Jackknife circled his desk again, looking down at the floor in thought. He needed to find the right words so that these kids would get it. Right, off the bat, they'd know what he's saying.

"That means using all of your gifts. If one of you isn't on target, then you are both off target. Wait for the other to catch up or ruin the child's dreams forever. People—use your instincts. Now is the time to make mistakes but more importantly learn and prepare."

The tone in Mr. Jackknife's voice became grave. He took his time, and his eyes moved from one child to the next as he spoke. "Put yourself in these kids' shoes. I guarantee, it will make you, and you, and you . . ." he says, as he points to random children in the class to stress this fact, "all of you . . . Olympic Jumpers. Learn from each student team evaluation. There are consequences for everything you do. That's it. Class dismissed."

The kids filed out of the room, jumped on their squares, and flew off to lunch in the cafeteria. Malia was feeling more confident. She was starting to understand how Dream Jumping works. Most kids' skills are on the same level, she thought. All the children agonized over being the leading D.J. duo. To whom much is given, much is required. Malia kept the saying in the back of her mind. Malia promised herself that next time, she would be ready.

CHAPTER EIGHTEEN

UGH, THIS LITTLE GIRL

This time, Micah was ready to Jump into Natalie's dream. "Malia says, let's do this. Are you sure, brother? Because if not, I'll wait until you are."

"Look, I said I am ready, so I'm ready, just trust me." Micah was shaking, but he was ready.

Micah closed his eyes and immediately Jumped into Natalie's bedroom. Malia smiled and said, "Hi, Natalie."

Natalie looked at Malia, then at Micah. "Whoa, hey, how did you guys get in here?" She bolted up in her bed, both hands balled into tight fists. She was ready to fight.

Having learned from his past Dream Jumping mistakes with Natalie, Micah was committed to making the little girl feel comfortable. "Shush ...slow down. We're here to help you become an actress. You want to learn how to act, right?

You're a good memorizer, and we know that you are always reading a play. You had one in your hand the last time we visited you." Micah paused.

Natalie's eyes watered up, and her lower lip began to quiver. She was on the verge of bawling.

"We're going to make it happen for you."

"I don't believe you." Natalie's eyes were giant saucers filled with tears. She surrendered her fists and unclenched and laid them on top of her floral comforter.

He watched as Malia moved close to the girl and sat on the very edge of her bed, keeping a safe distance. She didn't want to scare her within the safety of her bedroom. Her voice was soft, tender, and assuring.

Micah was glad that his sister had taken over at that point. He was nervous about how to soothe a girl's tears. Malia was a natural.

"Natalie, we know everything about you. We've been sent to you. We are here to give you the tools you need to help you achieve your heart's desires." Malia softly touched Natalie's hand. She felt motherly toward this little girl. Natalie wiped the tears from her eyes.

"How did you guys know that I've been asking for help? Did my teacher Mrs. Curtis tell you? Mrs. Curtis says that all you must do is say it aloud, and it'll come to you. So, can really you help me?" She was skeptical.

Micah answered, "Let's not get ahead of ourselves. How about we talk first, so we can all get to know each other?" He tried to take the lead from his sister's soft manner with the girl; however, he lacked her tenderness and sensitivity. He'd been an introvert his whole life.

Natalie sat on the edge of her bed, and her toes curled under her feet on the floor, slightly wiggling. They had her attention now. She nodded, yes, and they began to talk. Micah surveyed the tiny room, which looked more like a large closet, and it was practically empty. A shabby nightstand worn at its corners, a polka dot frayed beanbag chair, two-panel curtains patterned with pink roses on vines, and five posters along her bedside wall. Taped up in the middle of her poster collection was one of the child actresses named Quvenzhané Wallis the first African American child to star in the movie Annie. The poster had seen better days; its edges frayed, and there's a long tear at the bottom right corner. It was Natalie's inspirational poster, he thought. If a young girl could act in the role of a little girl, then she could become a movie star too.

He could hear muted voices on the TV stream down the hallway, maybe from the living room. He concluded it was a shabby apartment in a grubby building. This place for sure was not a fixer-upper. It needed to be condemned, he thought. No, it was more like a BLOWER-UPPER. It was in bad shape. No one should be living here. He shook off the vision of the building and turned his attention back to the girls.

"How do you know so much about me?" Natalie pushed off her bed covers and gave Micah a look. Micah understood that look. He had seen his sister give it to him many times. She was signaling for him to turn around so she could change out of her pajamas. Micah turned his back to her, giving her privacy. Natalie quickly dressed in a faded pink t-shirt and blue shorts that she had thrown on the beanbag after she dressed for bed that night.

With his back to her, he said, "Think of us as your fairy god-mother and godfather who grant wishes, except we really can't grant your wish. No, wait, scratch that." Micah's mind went blank. He was going from bad to worse. "Okay, listen to this. We will help you find the way to your dream. Do you get it now?"

"Yeah, kind of, I guess. Micah, you can turn around; I'm dressed."

Malia explained, "Natalie, we have powers, but the real powers are within you. Tell us why you want to be an actress?"

Once Natalie started to speak, boy oh boy, it was hard to get her to stop. Micah's brain whirled as the words poured out of her.

"My Mom had recorded five CDs, and she stopped because she started using a lot of drugs. She ended up going to jail because of that." Natalie hesitated. "My Mom said that my dad robbed a store and got caught, and that's that."

Micah couldn't believe a word she said. He looked to Malia, but her mouth puckered out, shush. She nodded and said "NO" in disbelief.

"Stop. Wait, a minute--did your mother tell you all this stuff? You're way too little to be all up in your parents' business. Shoot, Micah, and I hardly know any of our father's business, and we're three years older than you."

"First of all, Natalie snapped back, I'm not that little, and I'm a smart kid. My mother is my best friend. She tells me everything. That's how I know this stuff." Natalie's insistence made the twins believe her story.

Malia motioned for her to continue in case there was information that would help them with this assignment.

Micah understood that Natalie wasn't that LITTLE after all. She'd to grow up fast given what she's had to experience He settled in to listen to what he thought would be a long, long story. The kid was already acting as she told her story, and it was cool watching her.

As the sun began to peek through the rose-patterned curtains, Natalie's mother would soon return. They must be out of Natalie's dream in case she came in to wake her up. They've heard the dangers of being stuck between the vision and the child's natural world.

Micah didn't fully understand it, but he wasn't taking any chances. The twins reassured Natalie that they would help her, and the only thing they asked in return was that she trusted them.

The twins reappeared in Mr. Jackknife's classroom, and this time, the class gave them a standing ovation. They were shocked and embarrassed. As Malia walked to her desk, she raised a hand to quiet them. "Thanks, you guys, it's good. You can stop now.

On the other hand, Micah was goofy and loved the accolades. He bowed and smiled as if he had just received an Oscar for his Dream Jumping appearance. Mr. Jackknife raised his hand to end the applause.

Micah finally took his seat only because he saw his sister's face that said, " Sit your butt down now."

Mr. Jackknife asked the same questions he always asked when Jumpers returned from their assignments. "Okay, Y'all. What did they do right, and how can they improve next time?" He paused to wait for all hands to go up. "Come on, someone, anybody, challenge your minds." No one budged. Mr. Jackknife patiently waited. Micah believed the man was willing to stand there for the rest of the class period.

To Micah's chagrin, Jackson raised his hand. "Mr. Jackknife, I would like to answer both questions." Micah and Malia looked at each other, then at the idiot.

"By all means, Mr. Cannon, you have the floor."

Jackson stood, crossed his arms over his chest, and tapped his right index finger on his lips. "Don't get me wrong, they did an okay job, but I observed a couple of things."

Micah sensed some of the kids' disbelief at this dude because he was clearly showing off. Jackson wanted everyone to see him as fearless and intelligent.

Jackson continued, "I give them credit for entering the dream at the exact time. They can improve on their lack of confidence to encourage the child. At this point, I don't believe they can help anyone. They need to work on their delivery."

The classroom was painfully quiet as his words echoed within the silent room, bounced off the walls, and slammed into Micah's and his sister's ears. Mr. Jackknife cleared his throat. He always did that before he had something important to say.

Micah could hear gurgling phlegm spit up, and he swallowed it. Michal was grossed out. It gave him the shivers. EWE.

"Mr. Cannon, there's some truth to what you've observed. Nevertheless, 20/20 is hindsight." He turned his attention to Malia and Micah and said, "It's necessary to be sure of you and crucial for the assignment, the mission, so study to be ready."

The Crenshaw twins pretended they weren't bothered. Micah leaned over to catch his sister's attention. He gave her a wide-eyed stare that said, DON'T TRIP. She always looked calm on the outside, but Micah knew she was seething inwardly. He knew she would figure out how to pay back Jackson for his arrogant critique. Malia held her tongue and remained quiet. Malia would utterly humiliate him for making their lives hell, and Micah bet she would. He was long overdue. The kicker of it all was that Mr. Jackknife agreed with Jackson. Micah didn't see that coming at all. The kid drew a line in the sand. This meant war with that fool. Jackson's comments cut deep. That was the first time a classmate had gone for the jugular on any twin set.

The Dream Jumper Academy had a central area, an atrium, on the main floor in the middle of the school. The children's cubes surrounded the atrium on the second floor. A door from each cube opened to a balcony that overlooked the atrium where kids sometimes congregated, but it was primarily used for announcements.

After dinner that evening on the fourth level, Malia and Micah hung out in their cube with Tanisha and Mondarius. They overheard the Cannon twins bragging about Jackson's on-point review, which made the teacher agree with him. The brother and sister team were showing off in front of everyone watching from the balconies, and the kids were clapping and loving the whole bit. The two sets of twins walked out onto the balcony to see the spectacle.

Malia struggled, "It's so obvious they need an audience, and they're blatantly obnoxious."

Micah had to remind Malia, "They ain't worth it." He knew his sister would give in to her anger, and he didn't want the two to fight again.

Mondarius silently mimicked Jackson. He pantomimed the dude, which was so funny that they laughed aloud. The Cannons looked up and around to see who was laughing at them, but the four twins backed up to avoid the foolish brother sister team.

Tanisha whispered to her brother, "Man, will you stop? We don't need any trouble." He immediately stopped the antics.

Micah realized when he first met the Cannon twins that they were great-looking twins. It also struck him that the other classmates couldn't see past their looks to see their evilness because their beauty hypnotized and blinded them. That's why kids were always brown-nosing them. Micah was sure they used their beauty as weapons to manipulate people. A wolf in sheep's clothes, he remembered the "Little Red Riding Hood" fairy tale.

The two sets of twins can still hear the idiot being braggadocios. "Bri," says Jackson, "Did you see their faces when I read those clowns?"

"Dude, dang, you were fearless. I'm so proud of you."

"You do know that we're the chosen Dream Jumpers, right? Do you know that?"

"Stop asking me the same thing over and over." She rolled her eyes up. "Of course, I know it's us." Bri laughed. "We're the best, the greatest Dream Jumping team here. Period. End of sentence."

The two made an offensive display of ego, body slam, bumped fists, and cheered for themselves loudly enough to be heard.

"The Cannons, the Cannons, the Cannons! Yep, Y'all know who we are!"

Jackson topped off this self-adulated spectacle with a confident "Yes, y'all best believe it!"

"These pompous clowns really believe they are the chosen ones," Micah said. The others agreed with him.

The Cannon twins continued their high-five dance, with Moon and Star's peon sidekicks waddling around with them. "Cannons! Cannons!" They tried to keep up, but they were breathy and slow. Lots of kids from the balconies were chatting too.

Micah, Malia, Tanisha, and Mondarius couldn't watch the end of their victory song and dance. They closed the door to the balcony, but they could still hear the chanting inside their cubes and tried to tune them out.

"The atrium is only supposed to be used for special announcements. They took advantage of the open balconies to catch everyone's attention. The walls have an amplification system built into them, so that's why everyone can hear from inside their cubes," Tanisha explained.

"I want to know why they aren't in trouble for yelling and bragging and causing a scene," Malia declared loudly and with righteous anger. "Y'all know if that were us, we'd get in trouble and probably kicked out." They all agreed.

Malia and her brother weren't slackers. Realistically, they could be the top team. The glitch is--neither one wanted to be different. They only wanted to blend in for the first time, like the kids that no one bothers or notices. They accepted that Dream

Jumping was their true calling, and they loved it. That's how this journey started out, just helping kids all over the world. The Crenshaw twins were targets, inside and outside of the Academy. That was the one thing they knew.

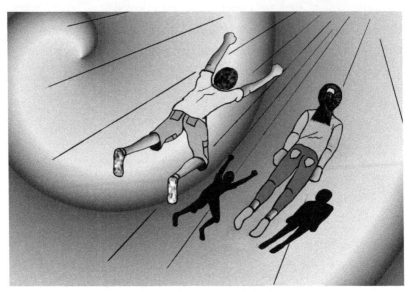

Micah's nightmare with Malia.
Illustration and Photography by Adrienne La Faye © 2022

CHAPTER
NINETEEN

BEING UNSURE

Micah and Malia hopped on their squares and flew outside to take in this beautiful afternoon sunset's last moments and reflect on their new assignment. Their squares glided them past the area where she fought Jackson. Micah peeked at the large tree branches where the demons tried to kill his sister. He chose not to bring up the subject.

His sister seemed to have temporarily forgotten about it. They found an isolated area on the west side of the island's shoreline. The twins set down their squares on the grass and rested under a billowing chestnut tree. The two were alone on this bright late afternoon.

"I am so happy we're Jumpers," Malia gushed.

"Yeah, me too," said Micah.

"Are you delighted you're a jumper, Micah?"

He looked away and pulled a long blade of grass out of the ground, placed it in his mouth, and attempted to use it as a toothpick.

"I guess you aren't going to answer me."

"Dang, Sis, you know I'm in trouble with flying, well, have good days, but mostly bad. I'm slow, clumsy, and I've failed at everything so far."

He threw the toothpick away, found a smooth rock, and threw it toward the water. They watched as it skipped along the sand and

"First of all, you're not a loser. If you were, how could you've done what you did when the Wrathtors attacked?"

"The kid I saw that night was large and in charge," validating his major accomplishment. "I know you have what it takes. You just do." Malia paused. "Look, I can't explain it, but you need to say it and believe it."

Micah sat with his arms around his bent knees, and he was lost in his self-deprecating thoughts.

"Micah, all I know is that you've got to get it together so that we can pass this level. Besides, I wouldn't forgive you if you gave up." Her words were sharp.

"What kind of pep talk is that?"

He gave her a look, and Malia could see a pool of tears in his eyes.

"Now you're threatening me. I thought you believed in me, and I should believe in myself? Great, no pressure, right?"

He tuned her out. Nothing she could say now would give him the confidence he needed. He didn't look at her during her endless pep talk. She vacillated between encouragement and threats, like an oscillating fan on the hottest day of the year.

This conversation was miserable for him. He felt lower than a crumb on an anthill. "Micah, I don't like it when you get like this . . .

I mean, it's like you're hopeless . . . Well, you're not. We are the Crenshaw twins who come from a long line of Dream Jumpers. Have you given any thought about how we're going to graduate?"

Micah finally gave up, and in what seemed like one long-winded breath, he said, "Well, yes! And DJAW is our only option. I'm not going to live full time with the father figure. And I refuse to disappoint Papa 'because he depends on us. I don't care about being the best Jumpers. I just want to get to the next grade."

His pain and fear flooded out of his soul in streams of tears like the endless flowing water of Niagara Falls that roars and crashes against its jagged cavern; however, Micah's cavern was the emptiness of his heart.

He saw Malia with her head down, and in his heart, she was at her breaking point. Then he heard the quiver in his voice turn into a wailing cry.

Micah wept loudly, and he didn't care if he was seen or heard. He cried about not knowing his mother and screaming about his dad hating them. The boy whined about Papa dying and leaving him. He complained about being clumsy and awkward.

He hollered about the future of their lives, his and his sister's, and it all rested on him because he was the weakest link.

They both sobbed until there wasn't a single tear left to cry.

"I'm sorry, Sis. I promise I'll do better." The boy's face was puffy and wet. He wiped away his runny nose on his jacket sleeve and rubbed his sleeve on his pants. He sniffled in the rest of his drippy snot, wiped again with his sleeve, and blinked away what was left of his tears.

He began to compose himself and looked up toward Malia. He was embarrassed that his sister saw him cry like a baby.

He knew she understood her brother's pride. She inched closer to him, leaned over, and wiped her snotty nose on his jacket sleeve too. As she did, they both cracked up in laughter.

"Hey, that's nasty. Why didn't you use your jacket?" Malia broke their somber mood, and both bust out into rolling belly laughs. That was the best medicine for the soul after a good cry, Papa would say.

CHAPTER
TWENTY

DOUBLE DODGE BALL

When Micah and Malia walked into the gym, a few kids ran over to them and asked if they wanted to play a game. They thought it would be fun to show everyone what they were made of.

Kids from the first level classes gathered in the gymnasium to play a simple game of tag to improve their hand-eye while flying coordination.

Then Jackson stepped forward with the idea to change the game to dodgeball. He took over the game entirely and insisted they needed to commit to improving their skills, so he started dictating who should be team captains.

Malia moved from the back of the group to the front. "I'll be a captain, and I want to pick my team."

Jackson paced and said, "Come on, losers, let's make this happen." Micah and Tanisha moved beside Malia, and Mondarius came to her side too.

"Let's do this right," said Malia, "and that means no cheating. Twin teams, ok? We don't want to split up our siblings."

"Let's make this more interesting," Jackson added. "Let's play double-dodge ball."

Malia and Jackson walked to the center of the gym and made up the rules for the game. Jackson counted all the kids in the gym out loud. "There are twenty-two kids in here, and we're going to need a couple of referees. That will make two teams."

Micah and Tanisha stood behind their siblings, waiting for their team leader to make it happen. Malia took over and said, "We're only using the floating balls in the game. All people must always be flying. If you aren't flying, you have been kicked out automatically. Let's pick our teams."

Everyone lined up on the red line. Malia and Jackson chose their teams. Albert and Alice were known to be the fairest-minded twins, so they were picked to be the referees.

"We're the M&Ms!" Malia announced, and her team yelled M&Ms. "We're the Cannons!" shouted Tanisha.

Micah thought, what a great name. He and his sister should have decided on a more menacing name for their team, but Malia loved that they would be considered the underdog purely because of their team's name.

As the newly appointed ref, Alice said, "I'll toss a coin in the air, and you guys call it. Heads or tails."

Albert asked team captains, "Heads or tails?"

Malia chose tails, which left Jackson with heads. Alice tossed the coin up, and everyone surrounded the medal, waiting for it to fall. It struck the floor with a metallic ring and spun. It took a few seconds for the coin to stop. Heads it was. The Cannons had won the toss. The teams mounted their companions and flew high, well, not everyone flew high, but they all were in the air.

The game was official, and the adrenaline in the gym was palpable. Both teams bragged about their flying abilities, daring the other side to make a move. It was clear from the yelling and taunting that this was not going to be a by-the-rules kind of game--this was war.

A considerable crowd had formed below. The word had spread that there was a game going on with Malia and Jackson on opposite sides. The younger and older children picked their favorite team to win. The gym was now a packed house.

Each referee held two continuously floating red rubber balls, which generally were for practice. Both captains had five sets of twins, which made two teams. Both teams were allowed to have two shots. Either side could throw the balls simultaneously and allow four balls in the air erratically and simultaneously.

The captains could match each team member against an opposing team member according to whom they believed could outmaneuver the other.

There could be only four members playing at one time, and that meant the others had to watch their teams on the sidelines.

The two teams flew high on opposite ends of the court, and all were ready for the massacre to begin. Before the game started, Malia told her brother about their game plan strategies. He drew an innovative diagram on his notepad for the M&M teammates. Malia reminded them to use their gifts in creative ways without cheating.

The game began, and Jackson's two team members attacked by throwing fastballs at the strongest girls' team. His team swirled balls without one student being hit, and then a shift happened.

The kids found their sea legs, and their flying capabilities promptly improved during this warm up period. Jackson and Malia matched up the four smallest members to fight first

She dodged the ball and flew up, extending her right arm, and caught it just before it hit the back wall. Then she retrieved the ball and shot it back at Jackson with the force and vigor of a kid not playing a game at all. Jackson sensed her anger and stepped up his game.

He started picking off the smaller kids first. He knocked down two and two more very quickly with a total of four of Malia's teammates.

Jackson's team were all pretty good flyers, and they had a flying formation going in and out of each other's paths, making themselves a more challenging target.

The M&Ms called a timeout. Malia had her team form a huddle. Malia gave them a new idea for the remaining M&M six members. She told them to double team the stronger kids first, so the others would get scared and surrender faster.

Jackson's team concentrated on one child at a time, and the M&Ms picked off five kids in a row, so now the Cannons had a total of five left. Micah improved, and he had new confidence in himself.

The rapid loss of his five players made Jackson start throwing balls even harder than before. Balls were traveling at high speeds in all directions, and the first to be knocked out of the game was a boy who no one thought would go first because he was so fast.

The ball hit the boy hard and knocked him off his square and down to the floor. Jackson laughed at this. It made him happy because it meant to him that he was the strongest and the best.

Malia flew down quickly to aid the child. She helped the boy to his feet and made sure he was okay. Meanwhile, Micah flew over to Tanisha and dared her to make a move. Tanisha didn't budge.

Malia looked up at Jackson, flew up to him in seconds, and balled her fists.

"Jackson, go on and throw the ball!" She shouted as she positioned herself in front of Jackson with her arm stretched out, waiting for the ball. He drew back his arm and made circular movements. He was winding up for his best kill and destroy throw. Jackson threw the ball and whizzed past her.

Malia then turned to Jackson and asked him, "Do you want to know how hard I can throw the ball?"

Jackson gave her his arrogant swagger and backtalk. "Dodgeball isn't a game for wimps. You're gonna get hit."

Malia raised her hand with the ball in it, drew back her arm as far as she could, and smacked the ball against the back wall. It imploded and stayed afloat, flat without air. She grabbed another ball and raised her hand to throw it but was interrupted by a screaming Mr. Jackknife.

"Malia, stop it now. Don't you dare throw that ball! Get down here now." Mr. Jackknife was upset about this so-called game. "Jackson, get your butt down here, too! Right now!"

Mr. Jackknife rounded up all the players and spectators and reprimanded each of them for partaking in such a hate-filled sport. It did not matter whether the children watched the game or played in it. He made them leave the gym except for Malia and Jackson.

"So, you think you are leaders?"

Malia said, "Mr. Jackknife, you don't understand what was going on . . ."

Jackson spoke up because he didn't want to get the blame for hurting that little boy. "Mr. Jackknife, its, and sometimes people get..."

"Stop right there. I did not say you could talk. First, you did not have permission to play any games. Second, the goal of the Academy is to nurture and develop your skills without hurting a fellow Jumper." Malia and Jackson stood silently and took their penance.

"You are to practice flying, which is all you are supposed to be doing. This kind of nonsense is not tolerated. Since you want to demonstrate your flying abilities, I have a job for both of you." Mr. Jackknife walked to the equipment room and grabbed two huge buckets, two squeegees, and towels.

"Ok, get over here."

The two Jumpers reluctantly rode over to the teacher and looked down at the buckets.

"Fill these buckets with soap and water, and I want you to wash those windows," pointing to the windows along the gymnasium walls.

Jackson whined, "How are we supposed to clean the windows and hold the buckets simultaneously?"

Malia didn't say a word, she figured it was best to keep quiet, but secretly she agreed with that idiot.

Mr. Jackknife was furious when he left the room. "I don't care how you clean these windows, but I want all eighty of them to sparkle and shine by eleven o'clock tonight."

The children who participated felt bad for the two captains because they were the only ones to receive punishment. They couldn't do anything about it, so they all figured it was best to stay out of it and let them do their job.

Malia and Jackson rolled their eyes at each other and fussed about washing the windows. Finally, Malia got her bucket ready, flew up to the highest window on her side of the building, squeegeed one window, and moved on to the next. She wished Jackson would make another arrogant remark, so she could show him how much he got on her nerves.

On the other hand, Jackson stared at the bucket and then kicked it. He realized that Malia was ahead of him in the punishment, so he raced to fill his bucket and tried to catch up with her.

They had to fly back and forth to the bucket on the floor, wipe the squeegee, and get more water to clean the windows. Malia was tired and didn't want to get into more trouble. The two never talked or looked at each other the entire time. Instead, they concentrated on getting the job done quickly.

While Jackson was washing the windows, he thought about the day he would get his chance to beat Malia at Dream Jumping.

Malia was angry and wanted to fight Jackson, but she knew that wasn't the answer.

She thought about how he "read them" in front of the whole class, and anger began again. She was going to pay him back by being the Best Jumper. Mr. Jackknife arrived promptly at 11 p.m. They were finished but exhausted, and they still wouldn't breathe a word to each other.

"Do you two still feel like you need to show off?" They hung their heads low and quietly said, No.

"Jackson, if I ever hear that you are trying to hurt anyone, you will not finish with your class. We will have a doctor evaluate your psychological behavior, and most likely, you will be expelled from school entirely." Jackknife was incensed with Jackson's lack of compassion.

"Why would you deliberately hurt a little boy? Why not take on someone your size?" Jackson still stared at the floor. He bit his bottom lip feeling awkward and embarrassed by Jackknife's shaming.

"That is not healthy behavior. There'll come a day when we all must fight, whether it is for a cause, family, country, you name it. If you want a fair fight, you best remember to pick on someone as big as you and don't bully anyone into it."

Then he wrapped it all up by saying, "I was proud of you two until this episode. You're going to have to fight soon enough. Get some rest and squash this nonsense. Put it to bed."

Both children thought about Mr. Jackknife and what he meant about having to fight soon enough. Did he imply they would have to fight each other or something else?

CHAPTER
TWENTY-ONE

WE'RE IN BIG
TROUBLE

The next evening, Micah's vision skills became present. He listened to the strange island sounds for the first time and heard them.

"Sis, come on, we better get back inside. It's getting dark."

They flew quickly to get back before the last bell that signals curfew, but his square seemed to pull in one direction. So, he leaned a little further in the opposite direction, yet his square wouldn't adjust.

"We're not going to make it at this speed!" Micah shouted. Then he realized what was happening. "We have to get out of here, right now! It's the Wrathtors!"

A strong gust of wind swept across their path. Malia grabbed Micah as his square pulled away from her. She held him upright. The last thing Micah needed was to fall in the middle of this windstorm. Malia had a tight grip on him as they sped quickly and maneuvered behind a dense hedgerow.

The hedgerow encircled them, and inside this bushy fortress were lush leafy trees of all sizes and shapes and lovely woodsy aromas they had never smelled.

A glorious scent of sagebrush, jasmine and freshly mowed grass filled the air. It was intoxicating. Malia led Micah to take cover under a centuries old Live Oaktree. A veil of Spanish moss flowed from its thick limbs like bolts of delicate lace enveloped the tree. It was an absolute refuge from that present and monstrous evil that lurks.

Micah once again began to whimper about his failures. He picked up right where he left off. He's failed repeatedly.

"I did do great the night of the attack, right?"

"Of course, you did. I saw you giving it your all, but you have to practice flying."

"Remember when we'd watch boxing matches with Papa? What did he always shout out to the losing boxer?" Malia mimicked Papa's deep voice.

Micah watched his sister imitate the old man. She was excellent at everything, he thought. Malia stood up and stooped slightly forward. She put her thumbs in a make-believe belt around her waist, just like Papa, and pretended she was watching TV. She had set her stage.

She bellowed out in her best Papa voice, "He doesn't want it! Nope, that guy doesn't want it bad enough!" She wagged a fist at the pretend TV. "He's not willing to go all the way! Look at him! You can see defeat in his face!"

Papa never understood why anyone would ever give up a fight.

"Dang, Malia, you're good. You can act just like Papa.

I almost forgot it was you and not him." They laughed.

"It's harder for me than it is for you." He got serious again.

"You're better at everything, and people pretty much like you, but for me . . ."

"You're ready," Malia said. "You have everything you need inside you. So, remember Papa and the boxing, and let's get pumped up."

Micah still wasn't convinced. He knew his sister didn't believe he was ready, but Micah was determined to fake it until he could make it.

Micah suddenly jumped up and screamed, "We gotta get out of here! They're coming now!"

Malia grabbed his arm! He could not see in front of him because his sight was focused somewhere else. He felt his sister pulling him, but he had no idea where they were going.

The sound of a hissing snake and ice-cold air interrupted their flight and threw them off course. Malia took them up into higher grounds, where the densely forested hills grew humongous trees and plants.

The bright moon helped illuminate different forest parts so Malia could see where they were flying. She found a small clearing in the woods and sat down on the soft ground.

Micah searched for the entities but saw nothing. He had more control over his sight this time because he could stay present in his surroundings.

"I think we're okay. They flew right past us."

"Micah, how are we going to get back to school without getting slaughtered?"

He'd almost forgotten about the Academy. "Oh no! We are in trouble. The Dean will surely expel us." He counted out their options using his fingers.

"One, we have to come up with a reason for why we are out here by ourselves. Two, we could tell the truth; the Wrathtors attacked us, and we got lost. Three, we're already on the Dean's bad list." He shouted out. "We're DEAD."

"Okay, calm down. We've gotta think this one through, okay?" She was square pacing back and forth, staying close to him. "Let's first figure out how to get back inside without getting caught."

It was too late. The twins could see Academy guards flying straight at them. Micah grabbed his handkerchief out of his pocket and wiped the sweat off his head, face, arms, and hands. They were face-to-face with six sentry guards.

One of the guards asked if they were okay, then motioned them to move forward.

"Hurry up and get inside. You do realize you shouldn't be out here?" "The Wrathtors almost attacked us. That's why we got stuck out here," explained Malia. "Why didn't someone come to get us? What took so long to find us?"

"Look, kid, you're not telling the truth. The Academy has been secured and locked tight since curfew, and we haven't had any alarms go off. We just received your signal. So, young lady, it's better if you don't lie and tell us the truth about why you're out here after curfew."

Micah saw his twin revert to the sister he'd known all his life.

She talked louder as her temper began to flare. "Mr. Guard Man, we're telling the truth, honest to God. So why would I lie?"

"Well, kid, that's a no-brainer. You'd lie about being out after curfew so that you won't get in trouble." He stared directly into her eyes. "Okay, let me ask a few questions."

"Where did you see them?"

"Where are they now?"

"Why weren't you at least beaten badly or dead?"

"Look, little girl, I don't have time for this, so you two need to get inside, and someone will attend to you soon."

Riding through the school's entrance, they were shocked that there wasn't a soul waiting.

The Oliver's were shocked that NOT one person hollered, screamed, or kicked them out of the Academy.

Micah whispered, "Let's go to our cube and wait for someone to come and get us?"

"Okay, maybe they didn't know we weren't in our room. Hurry, let's act like we were here the entire time." The Crenshaws sighed. They took the elevator so that they wouldn't be seen and tiptoed to their cube even though their squares had rebooted and were fully operational, and as far as they knew, no one would be the wiser.

They were hungry. Micah ordered first, "Five fried chicken wings, mashed potatoes, collard greens, and peach cobbler for dessert." He was famished. Malia filled her plate with catfish filet, carrots, hush puppies, mac & cheese, and chocolate pecan pie for dessert.

However, neither of them could finish their dishes.

Suddenly there was a knock on the door. Micah's eyes froze on Malia, and she mouthed to him, "Don't you dare answer it."

This time his knees wobbled and his throat was parched. "Hey Malia, it's me; open the door; it's us." He grabbed the door handle and pulled in Tanisha and Mondarius.

"Where have y'all been?" Tanisha chastised them.

"Yo, Y'all scared the bajezzus out of us."

Mondarius heartily declared. His twin raised her palms to chest level like she was in court, swearing to tell the truth.

"I swear we didn't tell anybody, so don't worry, just in case you don't want to share why y'all missed curfew?" said Tanisha, breathless.

Malia told them everything that happened and asked her new friends to give them an alibi, just in case.

CHAPTER
TWENTY-TWO

PAPA'S LETTER AND HUMILIATION

That night the twins dreamt they were back at home in the vault. They waited silently for Papa. Micah said sadly, "He ain't coming." The tiny door behind them creaked open, and TJ pounced in with envelopes in his mouth. They were happy to see their favorite buddy. In the dog's mouth were two letters from Papa. The kids took a seat in the tiny chairs and opened the envelopes.

They took turns reading their letters out loud.

Papa was a flawless patriarch of the family. In his letters, he wrote: Children, I know y'all are disappointed that I cannot be there, but remember, you don't need me there. You have everything you need inside of you. I know these are your best assets:

Malia, your gift is of another kind. You are a brave, generous, and thoughtful person but with a temper. You are a lot like your mother, but you have somehow managed to take these attributes to greater heights.

Your gift is physical strength and to encourage, protect, and nurture.

When you spot a flier posted on a telephone pole or at the corner store, you take the time to stop and write down the information so you can help look for lost children or pets.

You'd search online, and if there was no information online, you emailed the data to the neighborhood kids and their parents. You went to school and asked to make announcements over the school's speaker whether a child or dog or cat had been found or not. I don't know how you convinced the principal to do this, but you did, and you gained the respect of the children and the teachers.

The main thing I've noticed about you, Malia, is your ability to sense when people have a good heart, and you always try to mend people.

When your father realized your differences, he took you out of school so Grand One could homeschool you. He was embarrassed by your difference from other children, but these are your gifts.

"Yes, I did that," Malia agreed, "but I feel differently about that. I haven't helped anyone since being at the Academy; instead, I fight for us."

Micah, you are articulate, a natural scientist/mechanic, and a seer. I wish I could take credit for your intelligence. I have been entirely in awe of how you can make gadgets without hesitation. Micah, you took old Mr. Henry's lawnmower and found a discarded car seat, then made him a riding mower.

Now Y'all might not realize this, but that is different behavior for kids. You see things in a way that is beyond our understanding of children. That is your main gift, and you must nurture it.

You are the chosen Dream Jumpers. When y'all were in day-care, you were among the children who could be leaders. Y'all out-performed all the other children, and as you grew up, I watched your gifts develop.

The things that make y'all weird to other children are the same things that make you spectacular in the Dream Jumping World.

Y'all will break through the barriers most people impose on you by completely believing in yourself in your own time.

I think you two are great people. To sum it all up, yes, you are my CHOSEN ones.

Micah's confidence grew, and he felt more alive than before joining the Academy. Papa added P.S. at the end of his letter. He can no longer assist them or give them advice. They are on their own, which is why these letters had to be read in their dreams.

He explains that the old-time Jumpers are only allowed three visits while their grandchildren are in training, and he has used up his three trips. Check on Grand One, and do not forget TJ once you are graduated. He will be allowed to live with you at the Academy.

The children awoke to the sound of the monitor turning in their rooms. Dean Duckworth was streaming live into their cube. She got straight to the point.

"Malia and Micah, you've found yourself in another bad place; however, this is the worst by far. You have gone against every rule that you swore to uphold in the Jumper's oath. I can no longer allow you to get away with the type of behavior you displayed last night.

For one week, you are not to use your companion squares."

At that moment, their squares turned off. They had no power. It was as though the Dean's words controlled them.

Duckworth continued her lecture. "You've done things that could have easily been avoided if only you had consulted your squares. Neither of you has used your squares to ask for questions and guidance in situations that you encounter. During the next week, you will carry your squares everywhere you go to the cafeteria, the bathroom, and to class.

Do you understand? If either of you lashes out toward any of your classmates, that will be grounds for immediate expulsion, never to be able to return. Have I made myself clear?"

"Yes, ma'am." Answering in unison with tear-stained faces.

After their lashing from the Dean, the children moved in deliberate slow motions around their cube. Anticipating the humiliation that awaited them from the other children.

Micah walked the halls bearing the weight of his square and the humiliation it caused him.

Malia carried hers efficiently, but the shame she bore was the same as her brother's. She would bring her brother's square, but she assumed it was against the rules. This was absolutely the lowest humiliating point the twins had experienced since arriving.

Malia's temper flared up quite a few times, but she didn't utter one word. She kept her eyes peeled for Jackson, and the twins would turn in another direction to avoid him. The idiot was relentless with his taunts, and he eventually caught up with them. They swallowed their pride, no matter what insult he used to mock them.

They survived the week by going only from their cube to class and eating meals in their cube. During the week, they barely spoke to each other, let alone the other children. The week of punishment ended without incident.

CHAPTER
TWENTY-THREE

SUNDAY SCHOOL

Sunday came faster than either Malia or Micah wanted.

"Micah, our assignment is to watch from afar, not jump into her dream, okay? This assignment is supposed to help us get insight into Natalie's life."

Malia felt like she had to step up her game to prove herself because of how well her twin had done with the attack.

"I'm going to take notes on everything that happens today. Watch every move and reaction to situations."

"I'm kind of excited, are you too?"

"Yep, coz this is a lot safer than me flying around." The twins giggled softly. They watched her, but she could not see them.

Malia and Micah saw that Natalie's mother, Judy was tired. They stayed up too late playing games and watching TV, knowing they both had to get up early for church.

Judy dragged herself out of bed, made coffee, took her shower, and fixed a quick breakfast for them. Natalie was still asleep when her mother softly nudged her awake. It started to rain as they walked to church.

Judy didn't bring an umbrella, but it didn't matter because their jackets had hoods. By the time they walked into the church foyer, they were soaking wet.

A bright and happy looking young man stood at the door, "Good morning and welcome. May I take your coats?" he asked politely. "Oh, no, but thank you," Judy stuttered and took a service program from him.

"Please feel free to sit anywhere you'd like." He fanned both of his arms outwardly to the open pews.

Mother and daughter entered the middle aisle and sat at the end of a pew. Judy thought, not too close to the front.

Judy observed a congregation of diverse races but mostly African Americans families. The church had beautiful tall stained-glass windows on either side of the sanctuary depicting pictures of Jesus and his mother, Mary. The church was built in the early nineteen hundred, and it was as old as the rest of the Mount Baker district.

So far, so good, Judy thought; she would hold judgment until after the service. She may find it benefited her spiritually. Natalie watched the other kids throughout the church's sanctuary. She turned around and looked up toward a three-tiered balcony. The children there sat quietly in their seats.

The service always started with a prayer. The congregation sang a couple of songs along with the choir, and then someone from the group stepped forward to read a Bible verse. Natalie looked at her mother, whose face looked sad and deep in thought.

The twins watched them from afar. "Oh man, I feel sorry for both of them," said Malia.

"Yeah, me too."

"Her Mama must be remembering something sad that happened to her." Judy dabbed her eyes and nose with an old paper towel she pulled from her purse. She didn't say anything during service, but when she heard the congregation saying, "Amen," she felt comfortable enough to say it once or twice in a low voice.

A teenage African American girl walked up to Judy. She was slender and dark-skinned, sporting the latest Afro-styled hairdo and wearing a sleek two-piece purple dress with matching shoes. "Can your daughter come downstairs to our children's church?"

Judy turned to Natalie and whispered, "Nat, she asked me if you want to go downstairs to the children's church. You can go if you want to."

"Can you come with me?" Natalie hesitated.

"No, baby, you have to go by yourself, but you don't have to. It is your choice."

Natalie considered the possibilities. "Ok. I want to go. I'll see you later but don't leave me."

Judy touched her daughter's face. "Baby, I'm not going to leave you. See you soon."

Natalie followed the girl down the stairs. "I'm Rachel. What's your name?"

"Natalie," she quietly replied.

"This is your classroom, Natalie." Rachel pointed to an open door.

"Do you want me to stay with you, or will you be okay on your own?"

"I'm good. It's okay. You can go."

Rachel showed her into the classroom and introduced her to the children's church teacher, Sister Bowman.

There were about fifteen children from ages nine to twelve. "I'll come to get you when church service is over," said Rachel.

Sister Bowman was a pleasantly rounded woman with bright pink cheeks and blond hair. The Sister began the class by passing out four-by-six cards to the children.

There was a paragraph from a Bible story on each card. She asked a child in the front row to read from the card first. One by one, they each took a turn reading until they finished the story.

Sister Bowman asked the children questions about the story they read together. They enjoyed this teaching exercise. The children blurted out answers before being called on because they knew all the answers about Christ and his love for everyone on the planet.

The Sister sat down in a chair in front of Natalie and looked at her. "Have you ever considered that something out there wants to help you because you are loved?"

"No, Sister," Natalie shook her head. "I don't understand. This is my first time in church."

"Well then, Natalie, on behalf of the class," Sister gave a slight nod to the children, "we welcome you to First Church of Christ Congregational."

"Thanks for coming, Natalie."

The children greeted her in unison. Natalie blushed. "You're welcome."

The children's church hour was coming to an end, and before Sister Bowman dismissed the class, she said, "I want to remind you about this year's Easter play. It's time for auditions, and the play is set to start in three months. Anyone who wants to try out for the play should take a permission slip.

One of your parents needs to sign the permission slip for you to audition for the play. Okay? That's it for today. Remember, God loves you, and so do I."

Natalie waited until most of the kids left the classroom and slowly walked up to the sister. "Excuse me, Sis Bowman, can I have a permission slip?"

Sis Bowman was surprised by her question and blinked her eyes slowly. "Natalie, this is your first time at our church. Are you sure you want to be in our play?"

"Yes, Ma'am."

"Well, of course, you can have a permission slip." Sister handed her the paper. "Miss Natalie, have you ever acted before?"

"No, Ma'am... um, Sis Bowman."

"Honey, don't you worry. Most of the kids here haven't either."

As the girl turned to leave the classroom, Sister Bowman said, "Natalie? I'm expecting you to audition for the play, okay?"

"Yes, Ma'am, I'm going to audition. Thank you, Sister." Natalie responded.

The Sister watched the little girl as she walked out the door. Something inside her said that Natalie was going to be a star.

Rachel was waiting in the hall just like she said. She escorted Natalie back to her mother, who was waiting inside the vestibule to meet the pastor.

Pastor Konawa was greeting his parishioners. He was an Asian man with a soft voice and a pleasant smile. Judy surmised that he must have been about fifty years old.

"I loved your sermon, Pastor."

He took Judy's hand. "I'm Pastor Robert Konawa. May I ask your name?"

"I am Judy Roberts, and this is my daughter Natalie."

Pastor Konowa reached into his pocket and handed Judy his card.

"I hope to see you next Sunday. If you have any questions, please call me."

Mom and daughter said goodbye and began their walk home. "Mom? Do you like the church?"

Judy gave a slight smile. "Baby girl, I enjoyed the service, but I haven't been to church since I was a kid." She explained, "My Mom and Dad, your grandparents, took us to church every Sunday. But when I got older, I decided that I didn't want to go anymore, and I never went to church again."

"Why did you stop going?"

"I don't know why. Maybe I was trying to be like my friends who didn't go? Or maybe I was rebelling and needed my independence?" Judy paused in thought. "It might be all of those things. What I do know is . . . I'm happy we went today."

"I'm glad you took me to church. It's weird because I had a dream the other night that I was sitting in church and listening to a choir sing. It was this church!"

"Well, your dream came true! That's amazing!" Her mother acted somewhat surprised. "I guess it's good that we went."

"Sister Bowman gave us permission slips to try out for their play." Natalie handed the paper to Judy. She read it, and tears came to her eyes.

"Mom, what's wrong?"

Judy swallowed. "Nat, I'm happy."

Natalie was confused. Her mother was crying because she was happy. Adults. Go figure.

"Nat, let's sit down over here and chat."

It was on the same bench in Natalie's dream when the twins tried to convince her they were going to help her dreams come true.

"This is a starting place for you to act." Her mother explained. "I can't pay for acting lessons right now, so this is a great opportunity for you to learn about acting. It will help you get parts in local plays.

I don't know why I never thought of that before. You're a natural performer." Judy smiled as she continued. "You have an incredible ability to memorize movie lines. At first, when you were about three years old,

I thought that you were a little girl and playacting, the way kids do, but you never changed the way you are. Now! You're nine years old. And you didn't outgrow the playacting like I thought you would. It's in you."

Natalie sat quietly and listened to her mother's stories.

"I would like to think that an Angel brought us to this church, if for no other reason than for you to be in a play. Who knows? You can become an actress in all kinds of parts one day."

The excitement began to build within Natalie. I'm going to get that audition and be in a play. I know it.

"My dream was discouraged when I was little. I was passionate about being a singer. That was my dream, but no one helped me to get singing lessons, shoot my parents had the money but refused to pay for them.

Long story short, Nat, I grew up, got married, and I had you. My time to dream is over. Now it's your turn to do what you are born to do. If you want to act, I will find a way to make it happen."

Natalie's enthusiasm was geared up for the upcoming audition knowing that her mother would do whatever she could do to help her be an actress.

Malia and Micah saw everything that happened that day between Natalie and her mother. They were satisfied with the assignment.

"Hey, we're the best, aren't we?" said Malia.

"Of course we are! We were born for this." They did their usual celebratory high fives but added palm slide right into a handshake, a snap of their fingers, a double-fist pump, and topped it all off with a "whoop, whoop!"

The twins were pumped up too.

CHAPTER
TWENTY-FOUR

YOU MUST GO BACK

Mr. Jackknife sat on the corner of his desk, his long fingers folded together on his lap. He patiently waited for the applause and chatter to stop. He wanted to begin his lesson.

Malia humbly sat and looked around to see what the kids were cheering. Micah bowed, gave the class a thumbs up, and took in the accolades as he did the last time; he and his sister returned from the first Dream.

The class began to settle, and Micah took it as his cue to sit down. "Mr. Crenshaw. Ms. Crenshaw. I'm glad you're back. It is obvious everyone believes you have done a superior job."

The twins smiled. Malia watched Micah's eagerness to hear from the teacher what an incredible job they had done with Natalie.

Mr. Jackknife began. He stood and walked about the star in the center of the room. Malia knew that was his usual stance when he was carefully choosing the right words to reprimand someone. He stopped in front of Micah and glanced down at him.

"Micah, may I ask you why you were bowing like you'd won a championship? You must believe that your assignment is complete?" Jackknife raised an eyebrow. "Do you feel satisfied that you have done all you can to help your child achieve her dream?" Jackknife's speech was one long continuous flow of words that didn't allow anyone to interrupt him.

The children were motionless. When he got like this, he meant business. Somebody was in trouble, and Malia saw it unfold before it happened.

"YOU HAVE TO GO BACK," he ordered. "Your assignment is not over."

Malia shrank beneath the desk, trying to make herself as small as possible, hoping that Jackknife wouldn't pick on her. She only looked up when he stopped talking.

"The Crenshaw twins." His tone was commanding. He waited until he had their undivided attention. "Have either of you heard the term Dream Jumping Rules?"

Simultaneously, Micah responded with, "Yes." And Malia responded with "No."

Malia was sure she had never heard of the Rules. All the children were dead silent. None of them could believe that Jackknife was being so hard on them. He was telling them off!

The Mad Professor was what Malia would call him from now on. She felt her temper rise with this public humiliation.

"Before the two of you return to your Dreamer, you need to read the rules and carry them everywhere you go. The Dream Jumper rules are on the back of all Academy tablets. You all should know that by now." His glaring eyes moved back and forth from Malia to Micah. "You need to study and be more prepared for your assignment."

Micah was dumbfounded, but he had to ask, "Mr. Jackknife, how will we know when we've finished?"

Mr. Jackknife hesitated his answer to take in a deep breath through his nostrils. "You'll know when your child has made an advancement toward achieving their dream? You not only lead the horse to the water, but you must also wait for it to drink. You all have more work to do."

He chided the class for not being more perceptive. "I do not understand how you all forgot this essential part of your assignments. Let me break it down for you." He raised his hand and used his fingers to count out the Rules, starting with his pointer finger.

"One: You each must return to your child.

Two: Your child must complete one primary task in making their dream come true.

Three: I do not want to see your faces here until that task is complete."

Mr. Jackknife held up three fingers. Malia smirked. He looked like a boy scout in an oversized suit, ready to take his Oath.

"Got it? Take careful notes. Go now and return to your child. Help your child achieve one major goal toward their dream. You are dismissed."

The Crenshaw twins were the first to scramble out of the room. Jackson and his crew, along with the other children, busted out laughing. Even Mr. Jackknife had to laugh. He knew his stern talk was to improve their assignments.

He intentionally used the Crenshaw twins as an example to all the children. The way the Crenshaw twins shot toward the door and fumbled over the doorknob made everyone laugh. The twins, however, were not laughing. It rang in their ears until they returned to their cube.

Malia punched Micah on the shoulder. "What in the world were you thinking? Couldn't you just thank them and politely sit down, as I did? But noooo, you had to stand there and make a fool of yourself again, acting like you are Mohammad Ali. I should have said something the last time you pulled this crap."

Micah lowered his head. "Something took over me. It felt like it was the right thing to do. I'm sorry. It won't happen again."

"What has gotten into you?" She didn't wait for his answer.

"All I can say is it better not happen again cause you're not in this by yourself. When you look bad, I look bad."

"All right, all right. My bad. I wanted to prove that I am not afraid of anything." He paused to see Malia's response.

"Yeah, I get it. I do, but dang, enough with the theatrics."

"Keep in mind, Malia," he continued to justify his foolish behavior, "Everyone has to go back to their kids. It is not just the two of us who messed up."

She agreed, and with that, they both sighed in relief.

"Maaan . . . Jackknife sure was upset," said Micah, trying to deflect the reprimand.

"Yeah, he was. Now we must get this right. So, let's move on."

Micah reached for the notebook he kept in his back pocket, and the children gathered their thoughts about their subject, Natalie.

Malia waited for Micah to review his notes and began first.

"What I understand is this--until she does some acting or is taking lessons, we have to stay with her until she's successful at something. I don't know what exactly that is?" Micah lacked trust in the girl's ability.

"We have to put some events in place, so she'll keep working on her dream."

Malia and Micah watched Natalie from afar. She hadn't gone to bed yet. The little girl twisted her ponytail and held it for a moment while staring at her TV. Malia realized the child often did that when she was worried. It was her tell, a nervous gesture.

"Micah, remember we work together and in conjunction with the kid to help her achieve her acting dream? We have to get her to the play, and she'll do the rest."

The twins continued to observe Natalie until her mother told her it was bedtime.

It took Natalie only a few minutes to brush her teeth and put on her PJs. She slipped into her bed and pulled the covers up to her chin. She lay there wide awake and in thought. Micah thought she'd never get to sleep tonight.

The child turned onto her right side as her eyes became heavy with sleep. The twins had to wait until the right moment, the REM state, until they could jump into her dream. They carefully watched her eye movements until they saw a rapid flutter of her eyelids.

Then it was time. The twins closed their eyes and Jumped into her dream. "Hey, kid," said Malia. "How's it going?"

Natalie sat up and said, "Are you pretending not to know? Anyways, great news! I'm going to be in the church play. Mom and I talked about how she's going to help me become an actress. I'm on my way!" The little girl excitedly pumped her fist in the air. "Woo hoo."

"Not so fast, Natalie; slow your roll," Micah said. He sat cross-legged on the floor.

Malia spoke up. "When is the play?"

"I play the Narrator in two weeks, who leads the audience throughout the play." Proudly she stated, "I have more lines than anyone else."

"You're joking, right? You're going to read from a script?" Micah said this with exasperation.

Malia tapped Micah's foot with hers. She gave her brother a stare and a nod as if to say, dang it, shut your mouth.

"I'm not reading anything," Natalie explained. "I have memorized my whole part. Besides, there's only one role for a girl. I wanted to act and have lines, not just to hold the baby doll."

The twins smiled; they got it. Malia felt motherly pride for her petite chick as she readied her wings to fly.

It was Saturday and the day of the Easter play. Natalie was backstage and would be the first on stage when the curtains went up. She was a jumble of nerves and had already thrown up twice.

The twins watched her from afar as she nervously waited for the audience lights to dim. Malia had sympathy for the young girl who was about to make her first public appearance in a play.

However, the look on Micah's face clearly showed otherwise, and he finally had to speak his mind.

"I can't believe it. Natalie did a lot of big talk about being in the play, and she has her lines memorized, and now she's throwing up! She better get out on that stage and performs like there is no tomorrow."

"Micah, calm down. What's going on with you? Why are you so angry?"

"You know exactly what's going on. Jackknife chides us, embarrasses us in front have the whole class, and we're working with a

kid that may never do what she is meant to do. My guess is if the kid refuses to act, we don't get to graduate. I believe that is what is going to happen." Malia listened in silence to her brother's rant.

"I'm worried we won't graduate, and I don't want to disappoint Papa. We need this because we don't have anything else, Malia. Our father hates us. We never met mom because she died giving birth to us, and to make matters worse, Papa is dead."

"We still have Grand One," Malia tried to cheer him up. "You know she loves us."

Micah felt the frustration. "Malia, you know what I mean. Training to be Dream Jumpers is hard to do, and we can't tell Grand One anything about all this."

Micah's fears had transferred to Malia. She was now scared, too, and began to cry. She was afraid of her brother throwing in the towel. If he went down, she would also. She pleaded with him.

"Dang, Micah, we can't give up."

"Sis, I'm not giving up, but this is our reality."

"I know, Micah, but we have to believe that we have all that we need inside us. We are going to help this girl until she achieves one goal toward her acting dream."

Those words made her realize that they needed Natalie as much as she needed them. Malia wiped her eyes.

Backstage in the church, Sister Bowman gave Natalie words of comfort.

Sister Bowman says, "Don't worry about it, honey, to the little girl's relief. I'll take your place. You can be one of the shepherds. You will have plenty of chances to act in a play."

Natalia began to cry uncontrollably. She nodded to Sister Bowman while tears and snot poured down her red face, but she didn't want to be a shepherd. She wanted her mother to take her home.

The house lights dimmed, and the stage curtains closed. Sister Bowman walked out onto the stage in place of Natalie. The girl's mother knew something had happened and left her seat to go backstage.

Natalie looked like a baby. She sat on a metal folding chair, swinging her feet back and forth, and sniffling up her runny nose. Her face was stained with tears. Sister Bowman wrapped the girl in a blanket. Natalie was cold and nervous, and the quilt made her feel safe.

She was in a cocoon. She pretended. No one could see her.

Judy walked to her daughter and reached out her hand to Natalie. They left the church, hand in hand, and made the long walk home. Not a word was spoken.

Micah was beside himself, stomping around in frustration. "I knew it. I just knew it!"

Neither of the twins could believe their eyes as they watched Natalie and Judy walk right out of the church.

Malia turned to Micah in despair. "Natalie will never get back on stage after that disaster.

This play was her chance to show her stuff and prove that she was born to act. What are we going to do?" There was a long pause as she waited for an answer.

"Micah, will you say something? Please!"

"I don't know, Sis. I need more time to think. We have to regroup."

"No! We need to see Papa. We need some real help." Now Malia was angry.

Micah reminded his sister about the promise they had made to him.

"Remember what Papa said about us being on our own . . . we can't go to him again and ask for help."

"I know. I just forgot for a second." This was her problem as much as it was his. Malia felt resentment toward her brother. He was

precisely like Natalie. Micah had submitted to his fears too. He needed to be more compassionate toward Natalie.

Malia concentrated on her Papa's advice. Remember, you must adapt to all situations. Be changeable as the wind, water, and the air. You must bend with the flow. Have a backup plan.

Their problem was that they didn't have one.

CHAPTER
TWENTY-FIVE

THE LIBRARY AND
THE MANTRA

Malia knew they needed a plan for Natalie She had to be in a play, but they didn't know how to make it happen. Malia suggested they go to the school's library. The teachers encouraged the Jumpers to use the library, because of knowledge in books. There might be something in a book that could help them with Natalie.

The library was enormous. There were stacks of books from floor to ceiling, row after row. A thick red line painted on the floor led to somewhere. Micah looked down and beneath their squares are the words: "Toward the Keeper of the Books." They followed the line that ended at a tall wooden desk that reached up toward the ceiling.

The twins hovered up to the top of the desk, but no one was there. "Maybe the librarian is in the stacks?" Malia wondered out loud. She loudly cleared her throat hoping to attract someone's attention.

"How may I help you?" The voice of a soft-spoken woman came from behind them. The twins turned to look toward her, and Malia's heart began to race. The woman looked like her mother in the picture frame on her dresser at home. Her mind went blank.

Micah asked, "Are you the librarian?"

"I am The Keeper of the Books. My job is quite complicated."

Micah was impatient. He didn't want to know the difference because her explanation would take too long, so he quickly explained what they needed. "Our subject wants to be an actress."

Malia could not take her eyes off this woman. She was not old, but she was not young either, with a dark, clear complexion. She was quite pretty, thought Malia. Her face was slim, her cheekbones were sharp, and her lips were ruby red. She wore red oblong-framed reading glasses that framed her light brown eyes and matched the color of her lips. The contrast between her glasses and her bright eyes was mesmerizing.

Her slim mahogany fingers lightly tapped the computer keypad. "Okay, write this down." Before she could hand the children a slip of paper, Micah had grabbed his notebook and pencil from his back pocket.

She pointed to her right and said, "Go to the end of this row all the way to the wall. Turn left, and then go all the way to the end. There is the door that leads to the "James Baldwin" stairway. Fly up five flights. On the landing, there is an oracle that can answer your questions and give you the information you need." She smiled brightly; her red lips made her teeth look especially white and shining.

"Thank you, Miss Keeper of the Books," said Micah. He bowed his head in reverence to the woman who looked like their mother, as though she was a queen.

"Sis, what's wrong with you? I have never seen you this quiet."

"She looked just like our mother in the picture on my dresser. I look at it every day, not to forget what she looks like."

"Okay, well you're acting like you've seen a ghost, so chill. We have more important things to think about."

In the corner of the large stairwell stood a tall mahogany podium. On top of it was a shiny black slab that looked like a mountain cliff.

The twins stared at the black rock, not quite sure what to do next. "What do we ask it?" said Malia. Just as she spoke, the black rock lit up from within and emanated a warm blue glow around them. "How can I help you?"

Micah asked the oracle how they could help Natalie become an actress.

"Ask your squares to direct you to the book, The Jumpers World. You will find everything you need in it."

Micah thumbed through the pages of The Jumpers World and found something that piqued his interest. "Jumpers can manipulate a dream at any time and direct the dream to any place, building, and bring in essential people and tools that the subject will need to help accomplish their dream."

"Micah, if we can make up dreams for kids, then we can create a dream for Natalie to take acting lessons. We can put her in a play!"

"We're not only Dream Jumpers, but we're also dreaming creators, too!" he said. "How cool is that?"

Micah continued to read, "Jumpers must allow their subjects to be themselves, even when they make mistakes. It is important for children to learn from their mistakes and their successes. Life offers choices. As children grow into adulthood, they have the free will to choose how they live their lives." Micah closed the book.

"So, Dream Jumpers can create and direct the dream," he said, "but we cannot change the natural course of their decisions."

Micah continued to read silently, and then said, "Sis, it says here that we need to say a mantra every time we create scenes that aren't the subjects."

He pointed to the passage in the book, and the twins read it together out loud:

1. *If you believe it, speak it and do it, it will come true.*
2. *"Dream and dream, make your dreams come true. You have everything you need inside of you.*
3. *To fulfill your life's calling you must believe and never give up. So, dream big, live and your real life will come to you."*

"We have to memorize it," Malia said "I love it. It has a positive meaning. We should say it for us too, so we have belief in ourselves. This mantra is as good for us as it is for the kids we help."

Malia and her brother sat in the library brainstorming a plan that would help Natalie to become an actress.

"Where is the first place most kids learn how to sing or act? In a school or a church play!" Malia answered her own question.

The twins agreed that's where they would start.

The twins read the mantra from the notes Micah had written in his book. Their reality suddenly shifted, and they were floating above Natalie's family. Malia felt this shift was so magical, and there was more to it than just creating dreams.

"Sis, right now, I see us in the future. I'm not sure if it's sooner or later but being a Dream Jumper is going to open a new world for us."

They were on their way to create a dream come true for Natalie.

CHAPTER
TWENTY-SIX

THE LAST ACT

Micah watched as Natalie took the lead in the dream.

The next morning when Natalie awoke, she went into her mother's bedroom, laid down next to her, her arm propped up, holding her head, and waited until she saw Judy's pupils rolling under her eyelids.

"Mom, can you pay for some acting lessons? I need them." Judy pulled the covers back and motioned to Nat to climb into her bed.

Judy responded, "Yes, I told you I'm going to help you get a good start in life, even if I have to borrow the money.

We'll be alright, so don't you worry, ok?"

Micah was ready, and so was his sister. They were floating above watching.

The acting school was the greatest thing for Natalie; she soared in this venue. Micah was happy; it really helped her with her fears; she was learning how to act and loved rehearsing with the other kids. The eight-week lessons taught her how to use the tools.

"Hey Micah, I think we did much better this time because her taking the lessons made her have more confidence."

She auditioned for the lead role of Dorothy. She got the part, even though she was too young for it. That's how much she impressed the director of the play. She knew all the lines, and she could also act.

Micah talked with his twin, and they decided not to go back to school until Nat acted on stage.

The night of the play came. Micah was beyond nervous, and surprisingly, Malia was quiet and would not say a word. Natalie was backstage, and she started throwing up again. This time, Judy stayed in the back with her, and she grabbed Natalie by the shoulders, brought her chin up so her child's eyes would look into her eyes, and said, "Nat baby, this is your calling. Forget about proving yourself."

Micah said out loud, "Natalie, you can do this. Please don't give up." The kid couldn't hear him, but it made him feel better to say it aloud. He knew it was the girl's dream, and only she could manipulate the outcome.

"You'll always be my daughter, and that's that. "

Judy got a wet face cloth from the women's bathroom, wiped Nat's tears away, brushed a few strands of her hair out of place, kissed her on the cheek, and hugged her tightly.

"Thank you for believing in me. I want you to know if I don't do well, it won't be because I didn't do my best."

Malia and Nat stood and waited for the curtain to rise fully, as did her fellow actors. The curtain was up, and the audience started applauding. A hush fell over the crowd. Her cue was music played through the theater's sound system. Natalie stood on her mark. She heard people rustling about settling into their seats. Someone coughed in the back of the auditorium.

Micah stood up and started pacing, and Malia kept putting her hands over her eyes like it was a horror movie and she didn't want to see the ghosts.

Micah was speechless.

The lights came on and shone on Nat's face. Right on time, she let herself go, and the words flowed out of her. She was Alice in Wonderland.

Natalie received three standing ovations that night, and the play ran throughout the entire summer.

Micah was sweating, and he almost didn't want to return, but with all her courage, Malia convinced him that they had to go back and take whatever waited for them.

When Micah and Malia returned to their class, the students clapped but sat down, remembering what happened last time.

The class stopped abruptly to anticipate what Mr. Jackknife would say to the twins.

Mr. Jackknife stood up after the class's weak greeting, and he clapped loudly. That shocked everyone in the class.

"I want to let you both know I'm very proud of you two, and you've done the Academy an honor by serving at the level that you did. You have set the bar high. Excellent job!"

Micah didn't feel any better because of his insecurities and faults. He was worse than the kid because he hadn't faced one of his fears and had no plans of doing so.

CHAPTER
TWENTY-SEVEN

THE FINAL TEST

"Micah, hurry up! Read the test requirements so that we can advance to the next level, dude. I'm so nervous." Malia's teeth shone through her usually tight-lipped mouth.

"Hey, Sis, we've got to keep cool ahead to do this."

"Don't freak out on me. You how you get when you take tests, you forget everything until you calm down, so breathe."

"I'm good. I swear I'm good." She bent forward, gunning her companion square in the quick back and forth motions like she would drag race the others.

He read on, "It's a three-part test and the final exam of this term: History, Theory, and Jumping.

Micah thought this would be intense, and we must be our A game. Seriously, you hear me, right?"

"Of course, I hear you, silly; remember, it's already in us. Yasss."

"Yasss, you don't need to be competitive in line. What are you doing"?

"Leave me alone, you get ready as you do, and I get ready as I do."

Micah kept reading the instructions. "Okay," Malia said. "I will carry the backpack that includes the essentials: food and water and the map with the clues, and you take care of the map and keep us on course."

"Guess what? It is a scavenger hunt. I love a good clue, solving problems, and coming up with solutions. Ooo wee, this test is going to push us so hard that we have to stay focused."

"Hurry up, boy, and read the rest of the rules."

He cleared his throat, grabbed the paper sternly, and read through it.

"Okay, okay, I'm just saying…." They looked at each other and smiled.

ALL TEST RULES MUST BE FOLLOWED

1.   Their squares will verify whether the answer is correct or incorrect

2.   No exceptions are allowed for any of the rules.

3.   All twin teams have drinks and food supplied in their backpacks.

4.   No cheating is allowed, and it will automatically disqualify the

5.   The square will direct the Jumper when to advance. If the answer is wrong, they must remain at that destination until they locate the correct answer

6.   All tasks must be completed while flying on the square. They cannot leave their square and search for answers on foot. If any part of either twin's foot touches the floor or ground, that twin team will be immediately disqualified and asked to leave the testing

7.   Each twin team must complete every task before advancing to the next class level.

8.   Only the faculty members know the time allotted for each twin team to complete the test. This test aims to determine the skill level of each Jumper's unique gift.

"Come on, Micah, let's get in the last row of Jumpers and wait for the firing pistol to pop off to start the test. We don't need to be in front. Let Jackson and his crew show off, and we'll see who finishes first."

"I'm cool with that." Micah eased up next to her.

The teams lined up at the green starting line. Dean Duckworth hovered on the sideline with a firing pistol on her diamond sparkling companion square. She raised her hand high in the air and gave the Jumpers a pep talk. "Dream Jumpers! You can make your dreams come true. Believe it, speak it, and do it. Go forth."

She shot the pistol into the air. The Jumpers immediately flew to pick up their backpacks, and they were off, each team flying in different directions. This test was the deciding factor determining the trajectory for the rest of their lives.

Malia pulled out the map with instructions from the backpack. "Okay, Micah, let's first think this through. I have a backpack and a map. I think you should hold onto it since you are good at map reading."

"Let's not go too fast. We should take our time." Micah reminded her, and Malia nodded in agreement as he took the map from his sister.

"Okay? So, what's the first question?"

Micah read with apprehension, "What year was the Academy founded? HINT: Go to the 7th floor and locate the painting of the Academy by artist Rene Jacques."

"Malia let's fly straight up through the atrium to the seventh floor to bypass the elevators." The Brightly lit seventh floor. Micah envisioned the painting in his head before they got there. They found it and wrote down the year 1890 and the artist's name. They had answered the first question.

"Good call, that was nice and easy. I didn't see any other team. Maybe we're the first to find the answer," with a smile. "Come on,

Sis. We're not racing other teams. The is a test. It isn't a game. We are doing this for our family legacy.

We're up against ourselves." "Dude, that's even harder."

"Forget about that. We have to pass this test, okay?" "Okay, let's do this then. And let's not talk about winning again."

Micah studied the map. "Look, Malia, there are different sections. It says that we can follow the steps in order or choose which order we want to follow." He continued with his strategy. "We could do all of the easy stuff and then go for the harder stuff at the end."

Malia shook her head. "No, I don't think so. What if the order of the clues gives us more clues to the next section? We'd get mixed up because we went out of order."

He took a few moments to think about it. "First of all, we don't know if there are any more hints, but I'm with you about this place being in order, so let's follow the map's instructions and keep it simple."

The twins did a high-five.

Micah began to read all the test questions to himself. Malia stopped him. "We can't pass this test by reading every question right now. Let's take one problem at a time."

"Listen to this," he said, "The tests are designed for each team according to their expertise and gifts." Micah read out loud the three parts of their test. "Time, Accuracy, History, and Flying Abilities."

The twins agreed to stick with each task in the order provided. The next task: They needed to find a person or thing that needed their assistance somewhere in the Academy.

As Micah read off the task, Malia spotted Tanisha and Jackson. They seemed to be advancing quickly through their test. They did not seem to be taking this seriously. They had a carefree attitude and laughed while they searched for their answers

Micah and Malia, however, kept their focus. They were not going to exhaust their energy by worrying if any of the other Jumpers were doing better than them. Malia wanted to say something, but it was off topic from the test.

They were not allowed to chatter. It was just as though they were testing in the classroom. However, they could smile and nod to one another, which they do when agreeing with one another. They kept it moving and flew to their next location.

The twins began to follow their instincts and flew around the Academy. Malia pointed to something off in the distance, but it was too dark to see what it was.

"Micah, I think a person might be behind that post." They were in the east wing of the Academy's hallway. They approached the area with caution. It was pitch dark.

They saw a German Shepard that appeared to be hurt. The dog limped in circles. It whined in pain and lay down. Malia was a sucker for helping animals. She tried to get closer to the dog, but it moved backward. Then the dog took off, running down a spiral stairwell and went out of their sight.

Malia rushed past Micah. She looked back at him and frowned, "Why are you stopping? Hurry up! We have to find that dog."

"This may be the test for us to use our extra abilities and not let our emotions rule our logic," he replied.

"Well, use your sight and see what's ahead." Malia hovered around the small area where she had first seen the dog. She watched as her brother did his thing.

She couldn't see what he was doing, but she knew he had closed his eyes.

"Oh no, I don't believe this! They're here!"

"Who is here? Who, Micah?" She was ready for whatever he saw.

Micah pulled up next to her and cupped his hand to her ear. He said, "The Wrathtors are looking for us, in a barely audible voice. I can't see exactly where they are, but they're here for us."

"You got to be kidding me. We're supposed to be taking a test. How are we going to get through this with those creatures taunting us? Let's get out of here. Keep moving." She waved her hands in desperation. "Hurry up."

Malia motioned and led her brother further down the darkened hallway. She glanced at him but could not see his expression. There were shadows across his face.

"Come on! Hold on to my waist just in case they jump us." "What do you mean if they might try to jump us?"

"They can't get in here without the Sentry Guard, Teachers, and the Dean knowing they're here."

"I think I misread my vision."

"What are you telling me, are the Wrathtors in here or not?

"Well, I'm not sure, but logic says they can't be in our school. No alarm has gone off, right?"

"So, you're not absolutely, positively sure? Man, you're getting on my nerves. You cannot say crazy stuff like, 'they're here!' and then say that you may be wrong."

"Please . . ." Before Micah had the chance to finish his sentence, Malia blocked him with her hand.

"Okay, so Micah, we need to concentrate and find that dog. Close your eyes. Try to find the dog."

He did just that. His eyes weren't closed but still no reaction from him.

"Can you see anything?"

"No, I don't. Let's go back to the last place we saw the animal; it was running up the winding stairwell."

They turned around and kept a slow and steady clip as their squares moved up and up the maze, the spiraling stairs. Somehow, they have gotten lost inside the school.

Micah ordered his square to return to where they found the dog.

Micah said, "This place looks familiar."

They came to the top of the landing and cruised about the floor. The twins found a room with an open door filled with old furniture, desks, chairs, and tables rolled rugs. Musty smelling sheets covered the furniture.

Malia saw the dog that was now asleep on the floor.

They looked at each other and simultaneously said, "It's a trap."

CHAPTER
TWENTY-EIGHT

NO WAY OUT

The sheets lifted away to reveal the Wrathtors beneath them. It was not furniture! It was the demons! There seemed to be twenty or more of them. They began to screech and howl as they were exposed one by one. They encircled the twins, who were now surrounded.

Malia told her brother, "Hold on to me and don't let go. "She tried to break through them using all her strength, but they had formed netting around the room's perimeter. She could not push through them.

The Wrathtors closed in and captured the twins.

Malia came first, and then Micah. They were in a dungeon. An iron cuff with a heavy chain clamped the ankle of each twin that led to a quarry stonewall. An iron loop hung from a railroad spike hammered into the wall. Their other foot was on their square.

The twins were frightened and in disbelief. The Wrathtors had knocked them out and might have taken them outside of the Academy, but they could not be sure.

"Micah, do you think we're still at school?"

"I don't know where we are. It's so cold and wet in here. We have got to get out of here. Remember we were warned in that stupid tunnel nightmare before we came to DJAW? I think we're in

the same place.

If I can remember, there is an exit. Try to remember our surroundings in that tunnel."

"Oh . . . yes!" Immediately, Malia saw the dream in her head. "I remember! This place feels just like a tunnel. We are not on the Academy grounds. Do you think they want to hurt us? I mean, why us?"

"They want to hurt all Dream Jumpers. We are nothing special.

We walked right into their trap." "What do we do?

Micah slapped his sweaty head with his palm, and a lot of water splattered off him. "Let me think. I need to think."

Malia was shocked and relieved that her companion square adhered to her feet. She looked around, and there wasn't one window in the small dark room.

"Micah, hey, are you alright?" There was silence. She started crying, "Say something, so I know you're alive."

"Yeah, yeah... I'm okay," the boy said. "I'm trying to think."

"I had no idea the Wrathtors would take Jumpers away from the school," said Malia through her tears. "This is worse than the night they attacked the Academy." She cried out. "Help! Somebody, please, help us!"

"Maybe this is a drill, like when we're late for curfew?" Micah thought aloud, unaware of Malia's cries for help. He was too deep in thought. "Maybe this is the real deal? No one has ever been captured and kidnapped."

Malia was out of her mind, scared and crying.

"We're going to get through this, Sis,"

Micah tried to comfort her with his words, but his mind was reeling. What's going on? How do we get out of this?

Micah's hands shook as he flipped through the pages in his notebook. He confidently air-paced back and forth on his square.

"We must have been given something to fall asleep and dream." He was putting together the events of the day.

"Sleep! We fell asleep!" It was an ah-ha moment for him. "We have morphed into a dream together, but I don't know if it's your dream or mine."

He continued to air-pace around the room, reviewing his notes, then stopped midair and smacked his forehead. "Doh! Let's ask our squares. Remember? We have been told we should never leave them and always ask them questions. Now, I understand why!" Malia's tears stopped, and she looked down at her square

"Can you get us out of here now?" No. Only you can help yourselves.

Micah asked his square, "Tell us what we're supposed to do now." Brainstorm. Continue to ask questions.

Micah had a lot of questions, and he quickly bombarded his square with every problem in his head.

"Where are we?"

You are inside the Academy in a dungeon used to torture prisoners many years ago.

"Can you see outside of our room?" I can see into the next room.

"Do you see anything in the next room?"

It's dark, and there are at least twenty-five Wrathtors waiting there.

"Wrathtors! Why are they waiting?"

They need instructions on what to do with you two.

The children panicked; this was the closest they had ever been to an evil entity. Micah asked, "How do we get out of here without passing the Wrathtors?"

"You're not asking the right questions," screamed Malia. "I'm going to ask my square questions."

She looked steadfastly at her square and said, "Tell us what to do, now."

No, only you can help yourself.

The door to the room suddenly flung wide open and banged into the wall behind it. The children were startled and screamed out in fright. A shapeless figure floated into the room. They could see

through the Wrathtor!

"You'd better leave us alone. I will hurt you! I swear it!" Malia threatened and screamed out.

Through the door was the dungeon's chamber room. It was a narrow circular room with a high ceiling. A square hole near the top of the cell allowed the Wrathtors to leave and enter.

A fire pit raged furiously and mightily in the center. Embers and smoke filled the room. It was so intensely hot she could feel the warmth even from this distance. Malia wondered if they had died and gone to the devil. The twins froze and were terrorized by the evil that approached them.

The Wrathtor floated around the room like a puff of smoke from the fire. It changed its shape to look almost human with a long face, two long, thin arms, and black hollow sockets for eyes.

Its mouth contorted into varying shapes of grimaces and smirks. Its stench was reviling. The children held their breath, turned their heads away, and closed their eyes.

The Wrathtor unlocked their chains from the wall and floated around their heads, laughing uncontrollably, and back to the door's threshold. One extended gnarly finger gestured for them to follow into the raging, hot chamber.

The twins nodded no, too terrorized to speak. A brute force came from behind and pushed the twins into the scorching dungeon chamber. She could feel the intense heat against her face. Giant spiders roasted on a grill within the fire pit. Malia gagged and threw up in her mouth and choked it back down.

She didn't think it possible that spiders this large existed. Its hairy abdomen was the size of her head with legs so long and spindly. It might wrap around her body like an octopus if it were alive. Spiders were her worst nightmare. Malia hated baby spiders, daddy's long legs, disgusting furry black or brown, all period, and roasted spiders on the spit.

Eckevil knew this about her.

Malia screamed so loud it scratched her throat. "What do you want from us?"

She stayed close to the door, realizing that it was better to be locked in the dark than to be in that dungeon of horrors.

Micah was by her side and held her arm. She took a couple of steps forward to shield her brother from the heat and the raging evil spirits.

"You will not get away with this! At this very moment, our military Jumpers are on their way to kill you!"

Echoes of laughter engulfed their ears. The stench of the burning spiders was ghastly. It was the smell of death. The fire was bright, and the twins squinted their eyes because of the smoke and heat. They tried to shield their faces with their arms, but the chains clamped around their wrists were too short.

Malia felt something drop on top of her head. She rolled her eyes upward to see what was there. A long furry articulated spider leg came down in front of her eyes and touched the tip of her nose. The Wrathtors were haunting her with shrill screaming.

She shrieked in horror and writhed her head and body to break free from the spider's grasp. Her heart pounded out of her chest. She was freaking out, screaming at the same time. She flung her head back and forth and tumbled down on the dungeon floor. Finally, her mighty strength kicked in, and with one whip of her neck, the spider flung into the burning pit, but her face hit the dirty floor.

Lying on her stomach, Malia felt her heart pounding against the dirt floor. She spits dirt from her mouth and feels something warm running down her chin. She wiped away the warm liquid with her hand as she sat up. It was blood coming from her nose. She could now feel it pulsating. "I think I broke my nose." Her face began to ache.

Eckevil, the Wrathtors' leader, floated above the room, silently watching them.

"I can't take this anymore! Stop it!" Malia's voice echoed off the stone walls and back to her head pounding with pain.

The entities broke into one long, horrific bellow of their call to war. Malia remembered hearing it the day of the attack.

Eckevil slurred and spoke, "... we warned you Oliver's not to come to the Academy, but you chose to ignore the warnings, and you will be punished for that. Take them and make them pay." Eckevil left the room.

Demons circled the room using their bodies and the smoking fire to darken the cavern room to a blackout. They first grabbed Micah, swooped under his arms, and dropped him onto a flat granite slab. He was held down, a burlap sack over his head.

A bucket of water dangling above him turned over and powerfully washed through the porous material. Water ran into his eyes, his ears, and into his mouth. He choked and spewed out water.

Micah coughed and tried to scream at the same time, "No! Stop it! No, don't do it!"

"Micah!" his sister cried. "Don't you dare show them that you're afraid and get ahold of yourself"?

With all of her might, she broke the chains from her wrists, and within a nanosecond, she was at her brother's side ripping off the wet sack from his head. The

Wrathtors surrounded Malia, but she didn't care. She promised Papa to save him.

Her body was dragged away and slammed hard on the floor as her forehead cracked against it. The room spun, and a whirling helicopter sound filled her head.

She forced herself to come out of this blackout. Malia slowly pushed herself to her feet. A tooth had been knocked out from her mouth and rested on top of her tongue. She spits it out onto the floor in front of her. She was bloody.

She knew that this was it, and they wouldn't make it out. The Wrathtors whipped their chains against her sore bloody body; the room went dark. She passed out.

She woke to find herself in the same dank, windowless cell. Her body ached. Her face was in excruciating pain. Micah was close to her on the floor and crying from the sheer terror.

Malia closed her eyes, and out of pure self-preservation, she slipped into another dream.

A beautifully manicured lawn framed an Olympic-size pool. Micah and Malia were wearing their swimsuits and standing together at the pool's edge; they would race. The twins dove into the warm water.

They shared a love of swimming. It was where Micah felt complete acceptance and freedom. They swam in unison, freestyle, left arm then right arm, took a breath, and swam freely with no restrictions, but there was no end to the pool. They swam for hours and miles.

She stopped to get her bearings, but she was lost and winded with exhaustion, so she slowed down.

Malia turned to find Micah, but instead, she saw Papa. He was having a great time, laughing, and splashing water on her.

She was out of breath. She spat water out her lips and wiped the water from her eyes. "Papa, how did you get here?"

His face began to contort and disfigure. His features were no longer that of Papa.

He stared directly at her, emotionless, bit off his bottom-crooked lip, and spit it into the water toward Malia. Blood oozed out the gaping wound. She could see his gums and blood that had seeped between his teeth. He was hideous.

"You're a failure," Papa said. It was his voice but not his face. "You are not my grandchild. You have embarrassed the Crenshaw family name. Look at you—acting like you did a great job representing me." His feeling of disgust came through his words and rang loudly inside Malia's head.

Papa's bitten off his lip, and it floated toward her. She was grossed out and splashed it away from her. She was stunned by his actions and his words of disappointment. What did I do to disappoint him? Malia's heart broke.

Papa's bitten lip morphed into an oblong table beautifully dressed in a linen tablecloth, fine white China, and shiny new silverware placed perfectly around each place setting. A huge, juicy turkey on a platter sat in the middle of the table, was a carving knife was placed alongside the turkey. She smelled the fantastic food emanating in the air.

"I hate you, Malia. I wish you and your brother died instead of my beautiful daughter. You are both disinherited and no longer bear the family name."

He pushed the table over, not giving a thought to all the beautiful dinnerware on top of it, nor the turkey or its carving knife. Malia watched in horror as the blade flew into the air and spun like an airplane out of gas directly into the chest of her Papa. She blacked out and was woken by Micah calling her name.

"Malia wakes up! You've got to wake up!" Micah knelt next to her. She couldn't recognize where they were, only that they were nestled in a field of poppies.

"Micah, were you in that dream with Papa, too?"

"I was, but I only could watch. My voice was muted when Papa showed up. Listen, I've been thinking, we are Dream Jumpers and have learned how to control other people's dreams. Well, why can't we control who enters our dreams too? We have the power to keep the Wrathtors out of our dreams."

"More like nightmares. I don't get it. What are you saying?"

"It's part of our testing. These are our dreams, and we can control them!"

"Sis, think back to when we researched at the school library for Natalie. I read the passage in that little book. It went something like this:

"Your reality is your own, and ONLY you can alter it at any time." "Jumpers control dreams, which means can we control our own.

Micah shouted, "I fully understand how we ended up here!" He'd never shown such enthusiasm.

"What" The Wrathtors haven't kidnaped us? Our minds kidnapped us?" said Malia, beginning to catch on to what her brother was saying. "We're the only ones who can make our destiny come true. We must believe in ourselves. We are as good as everyone else."

Malia began to think about Serena Williams, who said she always knew she'd be the best tennis player. She believed it. She became it.

"Yea, that's right! You've got it!" he exclaimed. "I never believed it in my heart, but those words better be real to us because we are Dream Jumpers, and it is what we do."

"Are you saying the Wrathtors kidnapped us because, in our hearts, we had stopped believing in ourselves?" Malia's eyes brightened.

"I felt like a complete loser every time I failed at flying or standing up for myself or you. It's hard to keep good thoughts when you keep messing up." Micah was giddy at this point.

"Let's say the mantra," said Malia as she grabbed her brother's hand.

If you believe it, speak it and do it, it will come true.

"Dream and dream, make your dreams come true. You have everything you need inside of you.

To fulfill your life's calling, you must believe and never give up. So, dream big, live, and your real life will come to you."

Their dream ended, and so did the test. Belief in themselves made it just that easy. The twins were on the Academy's grounds.

She could see the school again. The GPS on the companion squares directed them up and around to the side of the building. As they entered the Academy, a table was set up along the right side of the long hall. Their counselors and teachers sat behind it. Adjacent to the long table were two chairs that faced the back wall. The twins wondered how long the staff had been waiting for them. What awaited them now?

Malia and Micah hovered down the long hallway. Sitting behind the table were their counselors, Mr. Little and Ms. Topperhead, and their teachers, Mr. Pointsetter and Mr. Jackknife. Each had a stern look on their face.

Mr. Little was the first to speak. "Children, please take a seat." He then commanded a TV screen to lower. "Start the video, please."

The instructors turned their heads to watch the replay of the test. The twins were startled to see themselves on the giant screen. They had no clue the test was recorded.

Each teacher reviewed the test section that was in their field of expertise; they each noted their successes and critiqued their failures and would inform them tomorrow of their final results.

And those who would move on to the next training phase and dismiss the twins.

Micah and Malia both knew they did their best and agreed that was what mattered.

The twins flew their squares back to their cube, and the halls were empty. "Where is everybody?" Micah asked.

Malia asked her square, "Where are the students?"

Some were still in the middle of their testing; others had gone to bed.

Malia and Micah were tired. They pounced flat on their beds, too tired to wash up and change into PJs. They quietly chatted about their horrible dreams, and slowly they fell into a quiet, restful sleep.

Malia and Micah hovered towards the cafeteria for breakfast.

They were rested but starving.

"I thought our dreams, nightmares, were real. That test was wild," Malia said.

"You ain't lying, Sis. I was freaked out of my mind."

"I think we are the first to finish the test because we didn't see many teams when we made it back," Malia said boastfully.

"Gurl, please, I hope we passed. That's all I want." Micah nodded. Inside the Founders' Hall at Dream Jumpers Academy of the World, a large sleek golden podium stood smack dab in the center of the stage.

A golden microphone was placed next to it. School colors festively decorated the hall. A very long slim antique table sat next to the podium filled with colored scrolled paper, each tied with a black silk ribbon.

The children watched with piqued curiosity. There was a low hush of chatter, and they looked all around to see who was there. Micah counted the sets of twins.

"There are only fourteen twins here," he said. "That's less than half of the first year's student body."

He looked at his twin, who was confident they had passed just because they were sitting there when most everyone else was absent.

"Yes, we made it!" she said.

Dean Duckworth walked proudly to the podium and patiently waited for the children to settle. She understood their excitement.

"Ladies and gentlemen, I want to congratulate you on doing an exceptional job on your testing." The students applauded and felt triumphant. "Those sitting here will move on to Phase Two of Dream Jumping."

All the children jumped to their feet, cheering in excitement. Micah and Malia gave each other a high-five and a brief hug. "I knew we'd made it!" she announced to their section.

Jackson and Brianna were there. They made it through. Tanisha and Mondarius made it also. Surprisingly, Moon and Star passed the testing too. Malia had gained a newfound respect for those two. She predicted the twins would move to Phase Two.

"Children, you should be proud of your achievements because this test was designed to separate the weak from the strong."

The children settled down into their seats to hear what else she had to say.

"Just so you all understand, we purposely created the test to be long and difficult. I am sure you students thought the test would never end." The children nodded and mumbled in agreement.

"It was designed to test your endurance, who thought well under pressure, and who could innately conquer their fears. We tailored it to your unique gifts to examine who can do whatever it takes to get the job done using your unique abilities. You'll find out, as Dream Jumpers, you will need to use your brains in unconventional ways.

Great job, everyone. I'm going to call your name for you to come up and receive your certificate for passing the first phase of training at the Dream Jumpers Academy of the World."

She applauded with a slow, loud clap. The students proudly joined in, believing they would make a difference as Jumpers.

"When I call your name, step up to receive your Phase One Diploma of Training at the Dream Jumpers Academy!"

The children were jubilant and cheering on each other. "We made it! Yasss!"

Dean Duckworth called out the names of the first set of twins. One by one, they climbed the steps to receive their certificates. As Malia and Micah walked to the podium, Malia smelled the sweet fresh aroma of homemade rolls. It reminded her of Papa.

Micah turned to his sister, giving each other a brief smile. "I smell them too," she said. Malia saw their Papa's picture amongst the others that hung behind the podium. That was confirmation that Papa was there, and the comfort of his spirit wrapped around her like a warm blanket. She wondered why she had never noticed it before. It uplifted her to see him. She finally felt at home with the Dream Jumpers.

No Dream Jumping team was awarded the coveted title of being the BEST DREAM JUMPING TEAM, and the children didn't care about that now except for the Cannons.

"Hey guys, congratulations," Brianna said as they flew away. "We didn't think you guys would make it this far." They then laughed loudly.

Micah stood and shouted, "Whatever, we do not care what you think, and don't worry about us; we're still here, and we aren't going nowhere."

There is a moment in life when you realize that you have grown, but you can't explain when or how. At this moment, Malia realized she'd accepted who she was, and this was starting place for what was to come.

THE END

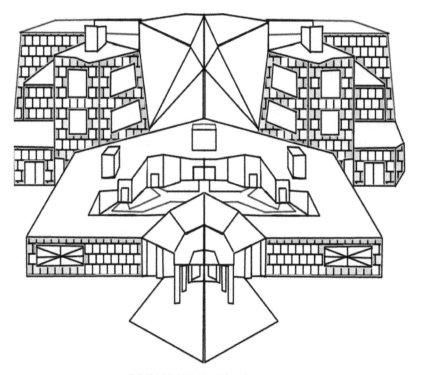

DREAM JUMPERS ACADEMY

Illustration and Photography by Adrienne La Faye © 2022

AUTHOR'S BIOGRAPHY

Adrienne La Faye is a painter, author, filmmaker, and community social justice art educator chronicling the African American diaspora in art. Her exceptional skills as a COLORIST are second to none.

She has been a full-time artist for over twelve years and was honored with solo exhibits, artist fellowships, and Seattle's Governor Mike Inslee art award. In addition, La Faye was awarded a solo four-month show by Mayor Ed Murray and has won numerous local and national grants.

In the book "Black Imagination," a compilation curated by Author Natasha Marin, Adrienne's writings were recognized; they were read in the audiobook version by Tony and Grammy Award-winning actor, rapper, and producer Daveed Diggs and Emmy Award-winning writer, creator, producer, and actor Lena Waithe.

Adrienne says Dream Jumpers perfectly combines her love of illustrating and writing into one genre that encourages children to become their best selves. La Faye loves children and has taught many how to paint and draw.

DREAM JUMPERS THE INHERITANCE La Faye's Middle-Grade book answers her calling. DJTI is the perfect gift for young readers and adults.